Praise for the Books of
Ellery Adams

A Killer Collection

"A very likable amateur sleuth . . . I'll be happy to follow Molly on her future investigations."
—The Romance Readers Connection

Ink and Shadows

"Lovers of reading and strong women will be impressed by this entertaining cozy packed with mystery, romance, and sisterhood."
— Kirkus Reviews

The Book of Candlelight

"Delightful . . . Adams has a knack for creating endearingly imperfect characters. Cozy fans will be well satisfied."
—Publishers Weekly

The Secret, Book, & Scone Society

"Adams's many fans, readers of Sarah Addison, and anyone who loves novels that revolve around books will savor this tasty treat."
—Library Journal

Books by Ellery Adams

Antiques & Collectibles Mysteries

A Killer Collection
A Fatal Appraisal
A Deadly Dealer
A Treacherous Trader (with Parker Riggs)
A Devious Lot (with Parker Riggs)
A Killer Keepsake (with Parker Riggs)
A Bidder End (with Parker Riggs)
A Fatal Fabergé (with Parker Riggs)
Mint Condition Murder (with Parker Riggs)

The Secret, Book & Scone Society

The Secret, Book & Scone Society
The Whispered Word
The Book of Candlelight
Ink and Shadows
The Vanishing Type

The Book Retreat Mysteries

Murder in the Mystery Suite
Murder in the Paperback Parlor
Murder in the Secret Garden
Murder in the Locked Library
Murder in the Reading Room
Murder in the Storybook Cottage
Murder in the Cookbook Nook
Murder on the Poet's Walk

More Books by Ellery Adams

The Charmed Pie Shoppe Mysteries

Pies and Prejudice
Peach Pies and Alibis
Pecan Pies and Homicides
Lemon Pies and Little White Lies
Breach of Crust

The Books by the Bay Mysteries

A Killer Plot
A Deadly Cliché
The Last Word
Written in Stone
Poisoned Prose
Lethal Letters
Writing All Wrongs
Killer Characters

The Supper Club Mysteries

Carbs & Cadavers
Fit to Die
Chili con Corpses
Stiffs and Swine
The Battered Body
Black Beans & Vice
Pasta Mortem (with Rosemary Stevens)

More Books by Ellery Adams

Hope Street Church Mysteries

The Path of the Crooked
The Way of the Wicked
The Graves of the Guilty
The Root of All Evil (with Elizabeth Lockard)
Fate of the Fallen (with Elizabeth Lockard)
The Deeds of the Deceitful (with Tina Radcliffe)

A Killer Collection

Antiques & Collectibles Mysteries

ELLERY ADAMS

BEYOND THE PAGE
PUBLISHING

A Killer Collection
Ellery Adams
This is a fully revised edition of a book that was originally published under the name J. B. Stanley, copyright © 2006 by Jennifer Stanley. Revised edition copyright © 2014 by Jennifer Stanley.
Cover design and illustration by Dar Albert, Wicked Smart Designs

Beyond the Page Books
are published by
Beyond the Page Publishing
www.beyondthepagepub.com

ISBN: 978-1-954717-64-0

Acknowledgments

Many thanks to Lorraine Bartlett for helping this book have a second life. Not only is Lorraine a talented writer (check out her books under the names L. L. Bartlett and Lorna Bartlett as well as Lorraine Bartlett) but she is also a generous friend.

Prologue

The potter's hands were wide with short, thick fingers, gnarled and cracked from a lifetime of work. Small burn scars crisscrossed the tough skin on the palms from feeding wood into the kiln. Dried clay was wedged beneath the ragged fingernails. Specks of it dotted the potter's apron and stuck like gray flies to his muscular forearms.

He reached under the cloth and drew out a ball of brown clay, looking it over for any signs of obvious impurities. He placed it on the scale and removed a few chunks from the ball until the scale read five pounds. He lumped the leftovers together and returned them to their shelter to wait under the wet cloth.

Slapping the ball on his wheel so that it would hold fast and create the right amount of suction, he dipped his fingers in a pail of cloudy water and drizzled it over the expectant clay. He began pumping the foot pedal on the wheel, and as it spun around, he moistened the clay until it became malleable beneath his hands.

As the potter centered the bulk, it lurched sideways like an unsteady drunk, and then rose upward like a giraffe craning its neck to reach a high branch. The wheel hummed softly as the potter worked under the light of a single bulb, the sounds of bluegrass music playing on the radio.

The clay was alive. Warm below his arms, it moved, stretched, and twisted. He cupped his fingers around its body, forcing the ripples to grow into a steady curve. He pressed more firmly at the base, and hips appeared as the weight of the clay settled onto itself. Around the rim, the potter pinched with one hand and smoothed the swelling sides with the other. Then, he let the pace of the wheel slow as he curled his hand around the neck of clay, pushing it upward in a gentle choking motion until it was a symmetrical spout, obedient to his will.

With a knife, he cut off the extra piece of neck and smoothed the insides of the opening. He stepped back and examined the piece, looking at the base, the round sides, and back up to the top where the centered spout emerged in perfect lines.

Satisfied, he slid a length of wire beneath the jug and moved it gingerly onto a stone slab where it would dry. This one would not get a face. It was too late in the evening and the potter was tired. He had made enough for today.

As he switched off the radio, he noticed the little lump of leftover clay peeking out from beneath the damp cloth. A new wedge awaited him tomorrow, and he didn't really want to unwrap the whole thing just to save this small bit. Still, he hated to waste a piece of clay. He paused, picked it up, held it, thinking.

His hands moved over it, hesitating. They weren't sure what they were supposed to do. Without the wheel, things were uncertain. Pieces could become anything—imperfect, irregular.

The potter smoothed the lump into a rounded body, and then applied pressure until he'd made a thick neck with one hand, widening a round head with the other. He pinched out two long, rounded ears, and pulled forward a small nose and cheeks. Dipping his hands into the water, he smoothed the body and pushed out a swollen hump to become the back and the hind leg, then pulled out two long, identical front legs from the clay below the head. With a wooden carving stick, he traced an upright cottontail on the base of the back leg, drew paws into the little feet, and made a triangular nose, winking eyes, a grinning mouth, and six whiskers. Lastly, he carved his initials and a number onto the base.

The potter smiled, flicking away any flecks of clay from around the last piece of work he would do that night. He hid it far back behind the other taller pieces where it could remain a surprise until the moment was right.

The rabbit smiled back at him, sharing his secret among the crocks and chums, the pitchers and bowls, and the face jugs with their rows of crooked teeth. It waited for the time when the potter's hands would reach out with his brush and glaze its naked body into a cobalt the color of the deep sea. The clay was patient. It had waited hundreds of years to be formed; it could wait a little longer to be burned blue by the kiln fire.

It waited. But the gentle hands of its creator would never come again.

Chapter 1

It was quick, it was ruthless, it was in-your-face collecting . . . . Did people really go this crap over pottery?
> —Andrew Glasgow, from *Catawba Clay: Contemporary Southern Face Jug Makers*

"Time to get up!"

The call seeped into the dark bedroom and murmured around antique woven coverlets and a turn-of-the-century walnut blanket chest. It stared at the Dutch girl with the metal bucket in her oil painting of snow, reflected the sheen on the porcelain curls of a pair of Staffordshire dogs, and tickled the ecru page corners on a stack of leather-bound books. Finding no response, it accepted defeat and melted into the open mouth of a large cherry corner cupboard filled with row upon row of white-glazed pottery glowing with life in the weak first stripes of dawn light.

"Madam!" This call was loud enough to stir the silence of the room and awaken the sleeping woman. The gray tabby beside her burrowed a sharp claw into the woman's hand as punishment for daring to move a body part.

The door was flung open without ceremony and a rectangle of light from the kitchen burst into the room like an uninvited guest.

"Who do you have in there?" Molly's mother asked from the doorframe, and without waiting for an answer, asked the groggy feline, "Sophie, would you like some milk?"

The rotund tabby turned toward the voice and issued a small chirp of assent. Molly, whose nickname was "Madam" in her mother's house, turned over and buried her head beneath the pillow.

In the kitchen, her mother sang little ditties to her seven felines, cracked open cans, and distributed dry food into bowls. Cats meowed, fridge and cupboard doors were opened and closed, the microwave whirred and beeped. Then her mother was back, balancing something carefully in one hand and turning on the lamp with the other.

"Get up, Molly. It's time to go."

"I'm up, I'm up. What time is it?"

"Four forty-five."

"Four! This is insane." Molly sat up and pushed a strand of dark hair out of her face. "You are truly an evil woman," she mumbled.

"Get up. Sophie wants her milk, and she doesn't like anyone on the bed when she's eating."

Molly looked at the porcelain doll-sized teacup and saucer her mother held with as much disdain as she could muster. Sophie glared accusingly at her in return.

"I hope you realize that I am going to be crabby all day," Molly announced as she shuffled off to the bathroom.

"Yes, dear. But I'm used to you."

"Hrmphh."

• • •

It was a cool, predawn morning. Molly shivered and wiped the condensation from the car windshield. Beneath fading stars, she watched as her mother loaded some rubber bins stuffed with bubble wrap into the trunk. It was hard to believe that this was the beginning of what would become another stiflingly hot June day in North Carolina. Molly rubbed the goose bumps on her arms and climbed into the driver's seat of her mother's pearl-white Lexus.

By five thirty, they were merging onto interstate 85 South toward Seagrove, home of the Southern potters. As Molly sipped her warm sweet coffee, her mother offered her a banana. Molly crossly waved it away.

"I can't eat at this hour. The truckers are the only people crazy enough to be on the road, and they're probably getting paid much more than I am."

"The *other* collectors are out here too."

"Oh," Molly moaned, ignoring her mother, "I wish I hadn't volunteered to cover these pottery fair things. I *hate* getting up when it's still dark."

"They're called kiln openings. And once you've been to one, you'll be hooked for life. I know you!"

"Well, it was your idea to suggest these articles to *Collector's Weekly*, and now I'm driving instead of sleeping. My editor thinks a series on pottery is a great idea, and he never likes anything."

Her mother examined a minute stain on her teal cardigan sweater. "The collecting world needs to be educated about Southern potters, and you're just the person to do it."

Molly had been an English teacher at an exclusive private school for eight years when the job started to wear on her. Though people assumed most teachers worked a short day and took summers off, Molly worked long days, graded papers on weekends, and spent every summer teaching extra classes in order to meet her mortgage payments. After eight years, she felt that she had no time for herself.

Whenever she did have a few moments to spare, she spent them attending auctions and browsing antique shops. Soon she was submitting articles to *Collector's Weekly* for extra spending money, and when a full-time staff position became available, she jumped at the chance to get paid for doing what she loved most.

She typically wrote on the bigger-name antique auctions in the area, driving around Virginia, North Carolina, and South Carolina to snap pictures and interview auctioneers and bidders. Her articles featured detailed descriptions of the items that brought in the highest prices as well as quotes from satisfied buyers.

After covering the auction beat for a year, she noticed that more and more Southern pottery was appearing on the auction block and then disappearing at exorbitant prices. Knowing little about the subject, she asked her mother for a quick course on the world of Southern pottery.

She had received a pile of books to read, but her mother warned her that the written word could never compete with the real thing. Molly would have to meet the potters and see them working in person to fully understand why people went wild over their wares.

Molly's mother, Clara Appleby, had once owned a thriving antique shop. Over time, she discovered that she hated being tied to retail hours and dealing with finicky customers, so she switched her business and became a dealer in Southern folk art pottery. Instead of renting and maintaining a costly shop space, she now conducted business using a simple website and a "shop" located in the log cabin on her property. Customers could visit by appointment only.

Clara's own house was filled with pottery of all shapes and sizes and she was well known as an expert on all things made of clay. Molly repeatedly teased her that she bought more to keep than to sell.

"You have to go to kiln openings to get the pottery at reasonable prices. Dealers can turn right around and double their money by selling the pieces they get at openings on the Internet the same day. Plus, some of these potters only make two batches a year. That puts a big limit on supply. You've got to grab them fresh out of the kiln," Clara lectured animatedly.

Molly threw her mother a sideways glance. "Sounds like a scam to me. Dealers wait for those two kiln openings a year and go crazy, buying up everything the potter has, right? I mean, the potters limit the supply and the demand increases, causing normal people to get up with the chickens. Pretty clever."

"It takes a ton of hard work to make this kind of pottery. We're not talking about pansy pots or coffee mugs. These art potters may have spent ten years learning how to make something perfect come off the wheel. I can't explain it to you. You just have to see it for yourself. You'll learn to love it all—the kiln openings, the pottery festivals, outbidding someone for a piece you just have to have at auction. Trust me, it's a complete addiction! People will *absolutely* kill for this stuff, you'll see."

• • •

It took about an hour and a half to reach Seagrove from Hillsborough, and the two women pulled onto a dirt and gravel road matted with a plywood sign that read C. C. Burle Pottery in rough, worn letters. The narrow, tree-lined drive was already packed with cars and the sun had barely begun to warn the sky of its imminent arrival.

"Look at all these cars!" Molly exclaimed. She had expected to see a dozen at most.

"We're late," her mother scowled. "We are going to have a horrible place in line. Just park anywhere. Hurry, hurry!"

Molly squeezed her mother's sedan in between a makeshift row of pickup trucks and noted several other luxury cars farther up the drive toward a rusted metal barn. The mix of people gathered in front of the barn was just as interesting. There were men in overalls and others in button-downs and khaki pants. Several women wore frumpy flowered dresses, and others dressed in pants, sweater sets, and pearls. Molly felt comfortable in her white blouse and khaki pants—one of the standard uniforms worn to a casual Southern event. Her eyes, which had felt puffy and swollen in the car, now darted around wildly as she tried to soak in all the details.

"I'm going to look over the pottery. Get in line," her mother hissed urgently and prodded her forward. Molly walked quickly up the drive to a patch of scraggly grass located between the barn and the potter's workshop.

She got in line behind the small cluster of buyers who appeared to be calmly chatting next to a rope. The thin strip of twine served as the divider between the customers and the three tables loaded with pottery. Molly noticed that the calmness on people's faces was likely a charade. Nervous glances were thrown back and forth between the other buyers, the tables of pottery, and the ticking face of a watch. Tension sat in the air like a low, heavy thunderhead.

"This isn't too bad." Her mother returned from examining the pottery. She counted out the twelve buyers ahead of her and smiled, pleased with their spot in line. "With two of us, we should easily get three or four pieces. Let's decide on what we're going for."

Molly followed her mother's eyes toward the pottery. In the young light, it was effused with a glow that only pieces made by hand seem to carry. Molly noticed a brown and white pitcher with a snake curling around the top. The snake's mouth was open as if to strike, revealing a red tongue and two rows of sharp white clay teeth. As she scanned the rows of face jugs, churns, pitchers, roosters, and crocks on the other tables, more people began lining up behind them, whispering to one another.

"I like that snake pitcher," Molly announced to her mother in a normal voice.

"Shhhhh!" her mother hissed apprehensively. "Don't say what you're going for or you'll draw attention to it. Then everyone will think you've noticed something special."

"Oh, sorry," Molly said quietly. "Which pieces *are* we going for?"

"Those two roosters on the table to the far right, that face jug with the crying eyes on the center table, and your snake pitcher."

Molly scanned the tables until she had located the two large red roosters with sharp, angular beaks and tails. On the center table, a jug decorated with a grotesque face leaked white glaze from its porcelain eyes. Molly grimaced.

"That's not very attractive."

"You'd change your mind if you sold it for five hundred dollars on eBay."

"I certainly would." Molly nodded. "So how does this work?"

"At exactly eight o'clock, C.C. will cut the rope and everyone will make a mad dash for the pottery. You have to have a good jump off the line—that's very important."

Molly giggled. She began imagining a wild animal stampede, complete with pushing and shoving, pottery smashing, and women screaming.

"This is pretty nutty," Molly said.

9

"Uh-huh. Just you wait," Clara said, then turned her head in the direction of a car with a powerful engine approaching the spot where they stood.

A large black Mercedes raced up the driveway toward the line of apprehensive buyers, forcing people to grudgingly step aside. The freshly waxed car stopped abruptly in front of the barn, spraying dust and bits of gravel into the air. A portly man with a shock of white hair slowly lifted himself out of the driver's seat and raised his hands to the watching crowd like a conductor ready to begin a symphony.

"All right, y'all can start. The Pottery Man's here now!" he called in a loud, brassy drawl.

"Who is *that?*" Molly asked her mother, who was now frowning.

"*That* is George-Bradley Staunton. He's a big-time collector and a full-time jackass."

"Oh," said a surprised Molly, for her mother rarely used expletives.

The jackass in question began moving up the line, shaking hands with reluctant men and flirting with all the women. A partially smoked cigarette dangled from his mouth and he paused to light another one whenever he began a new conversation. He wore a white linen suit with a peach shirt and tan leather loafers. He had loose cheeks and his neck was so thick that it seemed to have swallowed his chin. The formless neck and bulging green eyes gave him the overall look of a bullfrog. He dabbed at the beads of sweat on his forehead with a ratty, monogrammed handkerchief and moved toward Molly and Clara like a king receiving the acquiescence of his subjects.

"Well now, if it isn't the beautiful Clara Appleby! And this fine-lookin' lady must be your sister." Cigarette smoke was exhaled in their direction.

Molly made a visible effort not to recoil from the man's heavy hand, which was resting possessively on her upper arm. He leered at her and her mother, raking both of them from head to toe with his eyes while his thin lips stretched into a snakelike smile eerily like the one on the pottery pitcher.

"You two charming ladies must have gotten up purty early to come on over here and save my spot in line!" he announced, laughing. His breath smelled so strongly of tobacco that Molly almost gagged. She turned her face away and pulled fresh air into her lungs.

"G.B., we're way too far back for you," her mother purred with false sweetness. "You need to be much farther up to get the good stuff."

"Young missy," he said, offering Molly a dough-like, clammy hand, "I am George-Bradley Sherman Staunton the Fourth, but you can just call me George-Bradley. Are you a new collector I now have to contend with?"

"No." She shook and then withdrew her hand quickly and wiped it dry on the back of her pants. "I'm a writer for *Collector's Weekly*. I'm doing a series on North Carolina potters. This is my first kiln opening."

"Well, they're all as different as marbles in a bag. I hope you've got your racin' shoes on, girl, 'cause this here big boy is after some five pieces this mornin'."

"Good luck to us all," Clara said and turned away in polite dismissal.

With one last lecherous glance, George-Bradley Staunton moved up the line.

"Lord, what a slime! Does he sell used cars or lots of prime swampland?" Molly asked.

Her mother laughed. "He doesn't really need to work. His wife has a very large trust fund, but officially, he's a real estate attorney. He's got 'Esquire' on his cards along with that mouthful of a name."

"He oughta have 'Sewer Breath, Esquire' on them instead."

"Oh, he's a sleaze, there's no doubt about it, but he's got the premier pottery collection of central North Carolina, next to that man at the front of the line." Clara jerked a thumb toward a nervous-looking middle-aged man wearing a red and white checked shirt tucked into jeans.

"Who is he?" Molly asked.

"He has an odd name. Hillary Keane. He's the first one on the scene at any major kiln opening."

Molly observed Keane as he struggled to take off his silver spectacles. His hands looked swollen and gnarled, as if crooked branches had replaced the fingers and the knuckles had been transformed into wrinkled walnuts. Awkwardly, Keane removed his glasses and tried to clean them against his shirt, but dropped them helplessly on the ground instead. The woman next to him retrieved them, and he gave her an embarrassed smile. Fumbling, Keane replaced the glasses on his narrow nose and cast a cautious glance to the left and right before once again fixing his anxious eyes on the pottery.

"Anyway," Clara returned to the original subject of their conversation, "as difficult as it may be, everyone wants to be George-Bradley's friend for those rare days when he feels like selling a piece or two."

"Have you seen his stuff?"

"Not in person. I've only heard about it from friends. His wife is always at home, and she doesn't like pottery or the people in the business, so not many are welcome there. I'd give anything to snoop around that house. Did I ever tell you what happened at this opening last year?"

"No."

"Oh my stars, this story is a legend!" She lowered her voice. "Everyone was waiting for C.C. to cut the rope, just like we are right now. When he did, George-Bradley sprinted off to get some piece that he had to have. He knocked two people over getting to it."

Molly looked around at the tight spaces around the tables and considered the size of the current crowd. She thought about George-Bradley's wide girth. "I can see how that would happen."

"Yes, but one of the people he knocked over was an elderly lady, and she was hurt badly." Clara's face was solemn.

"How?"

"She broke her leg! George-Bradley shoved her so hard that she fell sideways in a twisted heap. She spent a week recovering in the hospital and had to hire someone to help her get around the house after she was released. She told everyone who caused her accident too. George-Bradley denied it. Never even apologized. And we all saw what he did with our own eyes."

"That is shameless!" Molly let a judgmental scowl fall on George-Bradley's barrel-round back.

"Forget about that greedy lawyer. C.C. and Eileen are heading our way."

The potter, wearing the traditional denim overalls that seemed to separate the potters from the collectors, moved shyly toward the line and greeted a few friends. He was in his late seventies and moved with the slow stiffness of a man who has spent dozens of years working in mills and bent over a potter's wheel. Molly noticed that the other potters were hanging off to the side, out of line, drinking coffee and humorously watching the tense buyers. One of them looked familiar.

"Isn't that Sam Chance?" she asked Clara as her eyes met those of a short, kind-faced potter with white hair and winking blue eyes. "It is!" Molly waved, and Sam held up his coffee cup in a smiling salute.

Occasionally, Sam Chance would go to area schools as a visiting artist. He'd set up a wheel and demonstrate pottery-making techniques to the amazement of the student body. Last year, he had come to Molly's school, and she had watched, spellbound, as he threw jug after jug for her sixth-grade students. The art teacher had arranged for several North Carolina artists to be guest teachers for a day. In addition to Sam, there had been a folk art carver who cut up logs using a chainsaw and turned them into alligators and giraffes. There had also been a storyteller who recounted Appalachian tales while having the class sketch the "feelings" her stories invoked. Molly had asked to sit in on each of these lectures and found them as rewarding as her students did.

"Do all the area potters visit one another's kiln openings?" she asked her mother.

"Only if they're friends or former apprentices. Most of these guys have learned all they know from C.C., so they come to show their support and to help wrap up the pieces after the sale."

Molly was surprised. "Wow. C.C. is older than I thought. For some reason, I pictured all of these guys as middle-aged or younger."

"C.C. is one of the last real traditional potters. He digs his own clay, makes his own glazes, and fires everything in a kiln he built himself. In fact, except for the ancient mule that he replaced with a tractor motor, he does everything just as the potters did it in the early 1900s. He's a piece of living history."

George-Bradley's bright white suit caught Molly's eye again. Done flirting with the attractive women in the back of the line, he moved toward the potters and began shaking their hands and slapping them on the backs with overblown gusto. When he reached Sam, Molly heard him say, "Sam Chance? What are you doing here?" He raised his voice like a bully on the playground, hoping to seek the attention of the other children. "Don't you have some *dinner plates* to make?" He laughed as the other potters eyed him angrily. "This here is art pottery, boy. The stuff that collectors are made of."

Molly was shocked. George-Bradley had called a man at least fifteen years his senior "boy." Sam's face was blocked by George-Bradley's expansive back, where sweat was beginning to spread through the thin jacket, so Molly didn't see the potter's reaction. Several of the other potters simply walked away, but George-Bradley rapidly cornered another, younger potter and began criticizing him on the weak color of his red glazes.

Eileen Burle, a soft-spoken woman in her seventies, saved the young man from further torment by asking for his assistance. She sent him off to the house and continued walking among the crowd handing out what looked like cookies from a wooden tray. Another, younger woman in her late thirties poured out cups of coffee or sweet tea.

Molly noticed that she was pregnant, but her freckled face lacked any trace of an expectant glow and her eyes stared fixedly at someone standing in line. Her gaze was so intent that she filled a glass of tea until it flowed over the brim of the cup. Blinking, she nervously cleaned up the mess and reloaded her drink tray in order to serve the waiting throng, which had now grown to almost two hundred people.

From her place near the front of the line, Molly couldn't believe how many people had congregated behind her. There were at least one hundred eager buyers wringing their hands and talking loudly with bursts of nervous excitement as the rope-cutting moment drew near.

Her mother introduced her to C.C. as he made his way over to where they stood.

"This your first openin'? You're in for a treat. My wife told me to go by the lottery system, where folks pick a number out of a hat, but this is too much fun to give up." He smiled, snipping his scissors in the air.

"Can you tell me something about that kiln, Mr. Burle?" Molly gestured toward the dome of bricks and wood sticking out of the ground a few hundred yards behind the pottery tables. It resembled an overturned ship whose rounded hull closely hugged the earth. At one end was an arched opening in the bricks that looked like a miniature railroad tunnel entrance.

"Call me C.C. Now, that kiln is called a groundhog kiln, 'cause it sits kind of squat against the ground. I've got to crawl on in there to load the pottery, then stoke it with wood, then heat it up good and hot for a few days. In the last couple of hours, we feed that fire like crazy and smoke comes pouring out the chimney there." He pointed toward the end of the kiln. "That's called the 'blast off' time. That's when you can look in at yer pots and they's as red as the devil, just a-starin' back at ya through all that heat."

Molly watched the pride flush his face as he looked over at his finished pots. He pointed at a gallon jug with a greenish, earth-tone glaze.

"That glaze is called 'Seagrove slip' and it's been made in these parts for more than a hundred years. My daddy made it that way and his daddy and his daddy did too. It's our family recipe."

"I'd love to ask you more questions after the sale, if that's okay." Molly told him about the pottery articles she planned to write.

"Sure, I'll take you around and show you all the tricks. You got yer eye on somethin' out there?" He looked in the direction of the waiting pottery.

Molly nodded as he winked. "Good," he said merrily. "'Cause it's time to fetch it."

C.C. moved over to the thin piece of rope, scissors in hand. The noise in the yard ceased. Just then, George-Bradley brazenly shoved his bulk between the potter and the first person in line, the nervous man named Hillary Keane. The man stared at George-Bradley, his mouth opening and closing like a landed fish gasping for air. George-Bradley completely ignored Keane's expression of silent outrage.

Smiling wickedly, George-Bradley leaned over to Keane and elbowed him roughly in the side. "My dear little man, what are you doing here? You know all the pieces you want are gonna be snapped up by yours truly. Why don't you just give up now and save face? I am the King of Kiln Openings!" Then, as if emphasizing Keane's hopelessness, George-Bradley dropped his empty cup onto the ground in front of Keane's feet and crushed it with an Italian leather loafer. He then stuffed two of Eileen's cookies into his mouth and chewed like a contented cow.

Rage drained Keane's face of all color. "Bastard!" he yelled, inhaling a great swallow of breath in order to release a stream of hatred at the rude collector beside him, but at that moment, C.C. severed the rope.

"Wait! Wait for me!" George-Bradley tried to bellow in protest, but his mouth was too crammed full of cookies to be heard clearly.

The crowd lurched forward as one body, shoving one another out of the way as each person moved toward a table. Molly headed for the nearest piece, the face jug with the greenish glaze and the white, crying eyes. As she reached out to grasp it, a thick, sweaty arm pushed her away so roughly that she lost her balance and fell to the ground. With a smarting elbow and stains on her shirt and pants, Molly quickly stood up again and looked around to see George-Bradley shrug his wide shoulders in mock apology.

"What a jerk," Molly muttered as she watched him disappear into the writhing crowd. She gritted her teeth and shoved herself forward, knocking into another man who was reaching toward the same piece. She grabbed the green face jug and began to fight her way toward the table where the snake pitcher still waited to be chosen.

Chaos reigned. Bodies collided and bounced off one another in every direction. Arms and hands reached out, desperately seeking to grab hold of the pottery, and angry curses were issued in sharp staccato among shouts of delight and disappointment. These noises were punctuated by gasps of pain as feet were stepped on, ribs were jabbed, or two pieces of pottery bumped one another too hard, chipping the glaze or creating cracks in the handle of a jug.

Molly darted through a small opening in the squirming throng, and though she was neither quick nor agile, she was determined to get her piece. She saw with relief that it had yet to be claimed. Pottery was being whisked away from the tables like it was on fire, and as she made her move to grasp the handle of the snake pitcher, she saw George-Bradley out of the corner of her eye, wrestling a large jug with the face of a devil out of a petite woman's arms.

"I had it first!" she protested, but he was too strong for her, and she released the piece and moved on to find another, her face a mask of anger.

The victorious scoundrel examined his piece for a millisecond with a look of pure greed and satisfaction, then returned to the fray. Disgusted, Molly looked around for her mother, spotting her just as she seized a red rooster from the back table. Their eyes met for a second, and both women lifted their pieces in the air, proclaiming their success before the crowd blocked their view of one another again.

As Molly turned to make her way back to the safety of the lawn, she saw George-Bradley's face beyond a trio of buyers arguing over a double-handed vase. Eyes darting about frantically, he searched for another treasure. Suddenly, he raised his head and howled in pain, his eyes bulging even farther from their sockets. In another flash, Molly's view was obscured, and then she saw George-Bradley stagger off toward the side of the barn, out of sight.

Curious, Molly held her pottery against her ample chest and followed. She poked her head around the corner of the sheet metal wall and stopped in her tracks. George-Bradley was leaning heavily against the side of the barn, his devil jug and another crying face jug resting on the ground at his feet. As she watched, he examined a tiny red stain on his peach shirt, his expression one of befuddlement.

Undoing the last two buttons, he exposed a roll of pasty flesh and rubbed at his flaccid skin with moistened fingertips. He repeated this motion several times, more and more slowly each time. His downcast mouth frowned in confusion. And then, his eyes lifted and stared off at something over Molly's shoulder. A look of surprise crossed his face, replaced by one of stunned realization.

Abruptly, a firm hand propelled Molly away from the corner of the barn and into the clearing. It was Clara.

"You've got to protect your pieces once you've got them, honey," Clara said, unaware of George-Bradley's odd posture. The two red roosters were already tucked neatly into one of the plastic bins, which Clara had strategically hidden behind the trunk of a pine tree.

The tight knots of struggling people had dispersed and only a few buyers remained around the tables, still playing a verbal tug-of-war over a vase or jug.

"That was crazy!" Molly said breathlessly as she collected her pottery. The bizarre image of George-Bradley examining his belly was replaced by the memory of grabbing her fabulous snake pitcher.

"Wonderful, isn't it?" Clara beamed.

"Actually, yes. I have to admit, that was like being on a roller coaster. Thirty seconds of pure adrenaline and it's still pumping."

Molly looked around for George-Bradley's bulky form, but he was nowhere to be found.

"Let's pay for our stuff and get something to eat," Clara suggested.

As they moved into the checkout line, Molly noticed that the tension permeating the air all morning had vanished, now replaced by a vibrant camaraderie. This was illustrated by a great deal of backslapping and cheek kissing among the fellow collectors. Buyers congratulated one another as if they had just returned from a dangerous mission in space, holding out their new pieces, admiring how each was made or glancing sorrowfully as a desired piece went home with another owner.

Molly felt rather smug and very affable herself. She chatted away with those in front of her in line and complimented a woman behind her on the beautiful brown and beige swirl tea pitcher she'd claimed. Molly held out her own snake pitcher and preened as it received praise. It was as if the pitcher were a newborn child instead of her first piece of pottery.

Clara's face was radiant with happiness. "It's just like a good auction," she said. "You're the worst of enemies while the things you want are for sale, but once it's over, you're all best friends again. It's pretty much the same group of people at all of these openings, so you may as well call a truce at the end of the day. They are your brother and sister collectors. They're practically family."

"And no one even looks at the prices." Molly indicated the tag tied to her piece. "Is every collector this insane?"

"Yes. It makes us a tight group." Clara's eyes narrowed as she noticed a green and brown smudge on her daughter's pants. "What happened to your clothes? You've got grass stains."

Molly was just opening her mouth to tell her mother about the appalling behavior of George-Bradley when a cry of "Help!" from behind one of the pottery tables rose into the summer air.

Molly craned her head to see that the man whose name was on the tip of her tongue was lying facedown in the grass, his body almost hidden by the other tables. He was completely still, his face an immovable white mask. A face jug with a snarling mouth and a pair of devil's horns was inches away from George-Bradley's outstretched hand. It was the very piece he had snatched away just moments before from the petite woman.

Clara drew in a sharp breath, taking in the shocking scene. She grabbed Molly's arm in alarm and then, just as suddenly, she relaxed her grip.

"Thank the Lord!" Clara exhaled in relief, her eyes glued on the pottery jug where it rested in the grass. "It didn't break."

Chapter 2

Perhaps an ideal future lies ahead when the world will be divided not by ideologies, but into those who make pots and those who buy them.
—Rosemary Zorza, from *Pottery: Creating with Clay*

For a moment, no one moved. Then a man bent over George-Bradley and checked for a pulse.

"It's weak," he said to no one in particular. "Someone better call 911."

From where she stood, Molly watched the man as he unbuttoned George-Bradley's sweat-stained shirt. He asked others to lend a hand moving the inert body into the shade until help arrived. Two of the potters attempted to pick George-Bradley up, but reconsidered. Instead, they carried over a large plywood board, which they balanced on the seats of three chairs. Their lean-to prevented the sun from shining directly onto the immobile form, but only made the paleness of his face seem more noticeable. Ten minutes ago George-Bradley had been flushed with animation.

Now, his pallid and expressionless face sagged like limp dough.

The crowd was silent. Once the potters had sprung into action, a few people began whispering in hushed tones. Ice broken, the entire crowd began muttering to one another in a tone of nervous excitement.

Nearby, a woman started crying. Molly noted that it was the same petite woman who had been holding the devil jug before George-Bradley wrenched it away. Molly turned to her mother and quietly told her about the incident.

"Her?" Clara pointed at the weeping figure. Without bothering to lower her voice she said, "That bag of bones is a total drama queen. Don't go feeling too sorry for her. She and George-Bradley have a shared *past*, and now that their affair is over they fight like cats and dogs at these sales. They also try to outbid each other at every auction just to get the other's goat. As usual, she'll do anything to get a little male attention." They watched as two men offered her tissues. Clara snorted. "Looks like she got it, too."

Molly examined the woman enviously. Short and thin, she looked elegant in a short-sleeved beige sweater, cream-colored skirt, and an abundance of gold jewelry. Her blonde hair was swept up in a glossy twist and her shoes weren't even dusty. Molly, who was a full-figured size fourteen, always wondered how it would feel to be as tiny and trim as this woman.

"She's wearing pantyhose!" her mother exclaimed in disgust, looking at her daughter's expression. Clara knew how Molly felt about herself. "In this heat."

That was a formal dismissal. Wearing pantyhose anywhere was an uncomfortable burden that the Appleby women avoided at all costs. Wearing them to a kiln opening on a June day in central North Carolina was beyond belief.

Before mother and daughter could continue criticizing the theatrical woman, one of the potters sitting next to George-Bradley gestured urgently to his friends. The second man quickly knelt and felt for a pulse on George-Bradley's neck. His eyes instantly grew round in panic and after a moment's hesitation, in which he glanced helplessly at the potter beside him, he began to administer chest compressions.

As Molly watched the two men continue to attempt to revive George-Bradley, the paramedics arrived. The crowd parted as the ambulance backed up in a series of loud bleeps, directed by one of the potters. Three paramedics hustled over to the prone figure with kits and a gurney. Bending over George-Bradley, they worked hurriedly, their faces set and completely unreadable. Within minutes, he was lifted into the ambulance. One paramedic continued performing CPR inside while a second briefly questioned the potter who had checked for George-Bradley's pulse. As the paramedic hopped back into the ambulance, Molly could see him look at his patient and shake his head. Then the doors were closed and the ambulance pulled away, its sirens eerily silent.

The crowd watched the vehicle progress down the drive. Despite the event, not many people had moved from their spots. Unsure of how to act, they simply waited to see what would happen next. Once the source of their shock was removed, they just continued checking out as if nothing unusual had occurred.

"Do you think he's all right?" some people asked without much genuine concern. George-Bradley may have been respected in person, but behind his back, tongues wagged.

"Didn't look too good to me. I heard he has some kind of serious diabetes."

"Really? Well, did you see him goin' at those cookies? I thought you couldn't eat like that if you had his condition."

"His condition is called 'Too Many Big Macs,' if you ask me," a woman said with a snide laugh.

"I'd call it too much smoking and beer chugging," added another.

One of the local dealers, a handsome man in his mid-forties wearing a denim shirt tucked into dark brown pants, approached the cluster of buyers.

"Oh, I know exactly what George-Bradley's condition is," he said importantly.

"Well?" a woman holding a large vase with a speckled glaze demanded. "What would that be?"

"When an ambulance leaves without using its sirens," he explained, "it can only mean one thing."

The buyers looked back and forth at one another, realization slowly dawning in their eyes.

"What you saw leaving here, my friends," the man in the blue shirt declared, "was a corpse."

• • •

The excitement of George-Bradley's collapse and dramatic departure had renewed the energy of the crowd. Gossiping at a mile a minute, men and women alike paid for their items and got in their cars, eager to be the first to spread the tale of his death around town.

Molly was shocked at their flippant reactions. She had just seen her first dead body, and she felt as though her mind wasn't working correctly. She couldn't seem to move her legs, and as the line moved forward, she simply stood still as other buyers went around her, paid, and left.

Finally, only Clara and Molly remained in the quiet yard. Clara comforted Eileen, who suddenly looked years older. Between the stress of the kiln opening and the shock of having one of the area's most notorious collectors collapse in her yard, the woman looked done in. Clara helped her pick up trash and gather the rest of the refreshments. As they worked, the women murmured together in low tones.

Molly felt that this was certainly not the time to interview C.C., but he caught her eye and waved at her to join him in the barn.

"I can come back at a better time," she offered once inside.

"Nah." He shook his head. "I need somethin' else to think about instead of folks keelin' over at my openin'. Come on, I'll show you around." C.C. seemed deeply relieved to have another subject to talk about.

C.C. showed Molly how he worked throughout the year in the cramped barn that looked like a small metal cabin. He had a fan for the summer and a space heater for the winter as his only comforts. The floor was mud-covered concrete, cool even in the summer heat. The entire length of the back wall was lined with tall wooden shelves used as drying racks and the rest of the room's accoutrements were reminiscent of colonial times. A crude three-legged stool was pulled up to a wheel that used foot power instead of electricity. An old door on sawhorses served as a table for holding blocks of clay wrapped in tight plastic to retain moisture. Wooden tools like spatulas or cheese knives were stuck haphazardly in chipped crocks near the wheel. Lined up on a warped tabletop were a dozen undecorated jugs that appeared moist to the touch. Every tool and piece of furniture was encrusted with clay.

"I just threw them this momin'." C.C. pointed at the jugs with a gnarled and chapped finger. "Couldn't sleep. Those new jugs that haven't been burned are called 'greenware.' See, I've turned them on the wheel but they haven't been in the kiln yet. They'll dry out for a bit and then go in the fire for a good, long roastin'. Come on in the house and I'll show you some old pieces."

Molly trailed after the spry older man on a gravel path that meandered behind the barn. Tucked neatly into the woods, the unpainted house looked as though it had always belonged in the copse of trees.

Inside, Molly noticed that the Burles lived a simple life. Their sparse furniture was easily twenty years old and the rusty hue of the shaggy carpet hinted that it too had been around for some time. Pulling pots off of a nearby bookshelf, C.C. showed her a jug with grapes on it that his grandmother had made out of rolled balls of clay and applied one by one to the piece that his grandfather had turned hours earlier. Afterward, she had incised some leaves and curled vines around the grapes to create a beautiful and delicate design.

Molly handled the piece gently, admiring its form, lightness, and the artistry of the grapevine.

"Can it hold water?" she asked.

"Tight as Noah's ark," C.C. answered. "After all, the Burles made this stuff for people in these parts to use every day of their lives. Local people made butter and cream in our churns and stored all kinds of foodstuffs in these crocks. I'm still tryin' to get used to the idea that people are buyin' my pottery just to look at it."

"What's the history of this piece?" Molly asked, holding up a piece that looked like two jugs stacked on top of each other with spouts sticking out in opposite directions.

"That there is a monkey jug. See, you put liquor in its bottom half and a water chaser in the top. These are actually two jugs fired on top of each other so they have separate compartments. Now, you get yerself a nice cup, pour some whiskey from this bottom section"—C.C. tapped the spout of the bigger half of the jug—"then turn it around"—he swiveled the jug so that the opposite spout on the top half faced forward—"then add yer water. You've got a cocktail party all in one place. Me, I like how the whiskey half is so much bigger than the water half."

Molly laughed as she admired the jug's speckled glaze. It looked exactly like the glaze on the pieces C.C. had put out for sale this morning.

"Could you tell me more about the family recipe?" she asked, pointing at the glaze.

"Now, that's fun. You get out your mixer and add one part powdered glass (we have a machine to break it up), one part ash from burned wood, and one part slip."

"Slip?"

"Slip is some broken greenware mixed with water."

"So you blend all that stuff and end up with greenish icing for your cake?"

"That's right. We keep it stored in a big barrel and dip a piece right into it. Gotta make sure there's no slip on the bottom or that pot will stick like glue to the kiln floor when it gets fired."

Molly examined a few more pieces on his shelf. She could see that even though the recipe for glaze was the same, each piece had a unique pattern of flecks, blotches, and drips. She picked up a beautiful crock that had a swirl decoration in green and beige.

"How do you make the glaze into that swirl pattern?"

"That's not the glaze," said C.C. with a smile. "You're lookin' at two different colors of clay. The secret to makin' swirl is somethin' I only share with other potters. You get yourself a wheel and I'll teach you."

"I think that would be wonderful," Molly said, and she meant it, but her few attempts to make pottery were disasters. Her finished products were wobbly, without the slightest hint of symmetry, and completely unimaginative.

When the tour concluded, Molly's head was stuffed with new details about the Burle family and their pottery. She was touched by the way C.C. handled each piece with infinite tenderness, by the pride he took in carrying on his family trade, and his excitement in teaching a new generation of potters the traditional methods handed down by men like himself for over a century.

C.C. had been creating useable art since the 1930s. His hands were arthritic, but they still turned perfect vessels and guided the hands of future artisans. Words were whirling around Molly's head and she was impatient to do justice to this gifted man. She couldn't wait to write her article.

After thanking C.C. and Eileen for their time and offering awkward condolences for the negative ending of the opening, Molly met her mother at the car. As the sedan kicked up dust going down the driveway, Molly looked back wistfully in the side mirror at the empty tables that had been laden with pottery earlier that morning. Her thoughts turned back to the sight of George-Bradley's body being loaded into the ambulance. The kiln opening had been more eventful than she could have ever imagined.

Molly examined the brownish flecks freckling the green glaze of her snake pitcher and struggled to put the memory of the paramedics loading the dead collector into the ambulance out of her mind. She leaned back against the soft leather of the passenger seat and glanced at her mother. "Where to?"

"Let's go to lunch," Clara replied. "All this drama makes me hungry."

Chapter 3

About all the potters that I knew lived to be up in their eighties, so I don't see where pottin' had killed any of them. Something's gonna take you away from here sometime or another anyway!
—Burlon Craig, Catawba Valley Potter, from *Foxfire 8*

The Jugtown Cafe didn't look like much on the outside, but the locals and pottery hounds all knew that it was the place to eat when visiting Seagrove. Though it was between breakfast and lunchtime for most people, the lot was filled with cars and trucks.

Inside, pottery displays on high shelves lined the perimeter of the room. Molly and Clara were seated below a row of menacing face jugs with large mouths and chipped teeth. They got the last table by the front door, relieved to be in the path of outside air since the air-conditioning was set to subzero.

"It's freezing in here!" Molly rubbed her bare arms.

"Coffee?" her mother begged a passing waitress, who carried a stack of empty plates covered with brown gravy.

At the next table, four men were finishing breakfasts of ham, eggs scrambled with cheese, bacon, toast, and biscuits with gravy. One of them caught Molly staring and smiled.

"We had to roll hay today," he offered. "Makes a man mighty hungry."

"I must have gotten up this morning at your regular time," she said, saluting him with her coffee mug. "Don't know how you guys do it."

"It's been a hard summer with this drought." He shook his head, lines of worry sprouting around his eyes and the corners of his mouth.

Molly searched for something to say, but couldn't think of anything that wouldn't sound hollow. The lack of rain since last winter had put the Carolinas in the worst drought anyone had seen for over sixty years. Many farmers had lost all of their crops or had to put down their cattle because they couldn't keep them fed and watered. The clover and alfalfa crops had turned into fields of brown bramble. With the exception of the few well-irrigated farms, the summer crops were goners. Large amounts of hay were only available from the Midwest, at exorbitant prices, and the Carolina farmers who couldn't afford to buy it were selling or slaughtering their entire herds months earlier than usual. No one could remember a time when meat and produce prices were higher, and it irritated the Carolinians to have to buy their food from faraway states like California.

Life was so different out here from Molly's little subdivision in Durham. Only two hours away, her neighborhood was filled with two-car families who worked and went to school in air-conditioned rooms. They played ball in the yard and went to the mall, rented movies, and ate out twice a week. Here, men struggled with the earth. They planted seed or pulled forth clay. Their backs were bent and their hands were weary. Their faces were crisscrossed with lines, the skin turned into tanned leather by the sun.

Molly looked around at the other men in the room. Undoubtedly they worked in the local furniture mill for eight hours a day, their lungs breathing in thin air beneath the false glow of fluorescent lights. Their hands too, she saw, seemed to belong to those of much older men.

Returning her gaze to her own table, Molly examined her mother as she studied her menu. Tall and thin with dark hair, Clara had a regal presence that came from a mixture of intelligence, confidence, and good looks. She scowled and narrowed her gray eyes as she searched for their waitress, motioning across the room toward her empty coffee cup. Molly smiled at her impatience, her own gray eyes twinkling with amusement. She felt revived by the strong, sweet coffee.

"Tell me more about George-Bradley," Molly prompted after they had given their breakfast orders to the harried waitress. "You said he had a juicy past."

"It's not an uncommon story," Clara said. "Often, a collector will marry someone who has no interest in their partner's collection. One spouse can try to get the other interested by bringing them to sales or to auctions or by telling them about the incredible workmanship of an item, but you can't make someone feel the passion. It has to grow from the inside. I think people are born as collectors or they're not. You have to have the *gene*. George-Bradley's wife, Bunny, didn't have it."

"The gene?"

"Yes. You see, he'd go to sales and shows and she would stay home or go shopping. She never went with him on the road, and she hated every piece he brought into the house. I've heard this right from the horse's mouth. It got so they practically divided the house in half so that all of his 'ugly things' were in his half. She was born without the Collecting Gene."

"Well, some of those face jugs can be pretty scary. Not the type of thing to put in your guest room."

"True, but what happened was that George-Bradley spent more and more time with people who shared his passion. Especially women. That woman you saw this morning, her name is Susan something, she wouldn't normally be attracted to someone with George-Bradley's looks, but when you find a person who loves what you love, it can change the way you look at them. You form this connection that's deeper than mere physical attraction."

"So why didn't George-Bradley just get divorced?"

"Who knows? Bunny's always known about him running around, but she never sought a divorce either. Marriages are full of secrets. You never know what's really going on behind closed doors."

The waitress arrived with delicious crepe-style pancakes, eggs, and very crisp bacon, as requested. Molly poured some pecan syrup in a thin drizzle over the melting pat of butter in the center of her light and savory pancakes and licked her lips in anticipation.

Clara raised her eyebrows as she watched Molly pour, but refrained from saying anything about her daughter's eating habits. Molly was on the plump side with her round hips and an ample bosom, but she was still a lovely woman. Clara always marveled at her daughter's flawless and luminescent skin and the sweep of long, dark eyelashes framing eyes that always held a glint of amusement.

Such beauty and intelligence should not go to waste, Clara thought. "Now, speaking of marriage—" she began.

"Don't start," Molly interrupted. "I just haven't found the right guy."

"But you're thirty now. You'd better get a move on. I want grandchildren before you put me in the nursing home."

Molly sighed. "I'm working on it, but if you keep nagging me about grandkids, you're going to that home much earlier than you'd like."

As her mother fantasized aloud about where to hold the wedding reception, Molly's thoughts wandered to Matt Harrison, the marketing director at *Collector's Weekly*. She'd had a crush on him since the moment she joined the staff, but even after two years they had barely exchanged more than a quick greeting in the break room or a wave in the hall. Molly could see into Matt's office from her desk, and for two years she'd furtively studied his tall frame and watched his shy smile as he talked on the phone or worked on his computer.

As she wondered for the millionth time whether Matt had a girlfriend, her mother plowed full steam ahead on her usual litany regarding the family engagement ring that awaited Molly in Clara's jewelry box. Molly was saved from having to listen by the arrival of a group of boisterous newcomers who sat down at a neighboring booth. All three women were talking at the same time so that it was difficult to distinguish what was being said. They sounded like a gaggle of geese.

As they settled into their seats, it became clear that the loudest woman was speaking about George-Bradley. Molly and Clara's ears perked up.

"This morning, at C.C. Burle's opening," the woman continued, relating her story to her two wide-eyed friends.

"What happened?"

"Well, Trish said he just keeled on over. Boom. Landed right on the grass without hurtin' a hair on a single piece of pottery."

"Did he have a heart attack?" her friend asked.

"I don't know. Trish said they picked him up in an ambulance and took him away. He was white as a sheet in bleach, but that's all I know. He was stuffing cookies in his mouth like they were goin' out of style, that's for sure. With the shape he was in, it could have been anything. When Trish told me, I wasn't surprised a bit, but poor C.C. and Eileen."

The women all clucked in sympathy. "Did George-Bradley cut the line at this openin' too?" someone asked after a moment.

"Of course he did! Right in front of Hillary Keane. *And* Trish said he grabbed a face jug right out of Susan Black's hands. She was spittin' mad."

"I don't know who he thinks he is, that George-Bradley," one of the women snarled. "When I was first collecting, he took an old crock right out of my hands at a tag sale. He told me it was damaged and I wouldn't want it. Stuck it in front of my face and said, 'See? Look at all them scratches.' Then he put a different crock in my hands and said, 'Allow me to advise you. Buy this one.' And stupid me, I bought it. I found out later that the scratched crock actually had a poem written on it about the potter's wife. It was late nineteenth century and worth over a thousand dollars. I hate that man for cheatin' me that way!"

Her friends murmured in agreement.

"Still, I don't wish a heart attack on anyone." The woman sighed reluctantly as if that's exactly what she wished. "If that's what happened."

"Oh, we're going to find out," announced the third woman triumphantly, holding up a cell phone. "You know Randy, the guy I dated for a while? He works at Asheboro General. I asked him to send me a text message when he finds out what's goin' on with George-Bradley."

Molly and Clara exchanged looks. They were done with their meals and their plates had been cleared. Normally, they'd be impatient to leave, but a combination of the morning's events, their full bellies, and the opportunity to listen to interesting gossip rendered them immobile. They lingered over their cups of tepid coffee and openly eavesdropped.

After the women in the next booth placed their orders, one of them said, "I don't hear your phone beeping. Why wait for a text? Call that Randy and find out what happened."

"I already tried. I'm sure George-Bradley will end up being fine. He'll be back at the next kiln opening breaking the bones of little old ladies and pushing people like me into the dirt."

Clara could contain herself no longer. She couldn't leave her neighbors unenlightened.

"No, he won't," she inserted herself into their conversation with a conspiratorial whisper. "His days of being the rudest, greediest man in Asheboro are over."

"Really?" asked one of the women. She was practically drooling as she leaned forward to listen to Clara.

"Yes." Clara stood and placed a few dollars on the table for their waitress. "George-Bradley is dead."

Molly also rose, watching the women's faces as they digested the news. She felt suddenly uneasy. Shouldn't they all be feeling more than morbid curiosity? Someone she'd just met, that she'd shaken hands with and spoken to, was dead. A man's life was over.

The spark was gone from the day. Molly was ready to go home.

Above her head, the face jugs smiled crooked, sinister smiles from their lofty positions above the diners, their pointed teeth and slanted eyes gleaming sharp white from within the shadows.

Chapter 4

The best pieces of pottery bring out in most of us on almost overwhelming desire to touch, caress, and hold them.
　　　　　—Peter Consentino, *The Encyclopedia of Pottery Techniques*

The trio of women at the Jugtown Cafe thanked Clara and she and Molly finally exited the eatery. Outside, the June sun was searing the ground and the humidity hung like a damp washcloth over the sky. The car was stuffy and filled with thick air. It was a typical summer day in North Carolina, the kind that drained people of energy and made them seek the shelter of rooms with air-conditioning, or at least a ceiling fan.

"Let's take the slow way back," Clara suggested as she rummaged around in the side pocket of her purse for her driving glasses. Replete with her tasty lunch, Molly eased the passenger seat back and stretched out her long legs.

Avoiding the interstates, the "slow way" took them through flat farmland and quirky crossroads following a crooked trail from Seagrove to Pittsboro, which was just south of Chapel Hill. Clara always drove home this way if she wasn't pressed for time. She enjoyed the rural scenery and the lack of large trucks and other noisy traffic.

They passed dozens of pottery shops on the way and Molly noted how different the signs for the potteries were. Some had been like C.C.'s—simple, hand-painted lettering on a white wood board. Some were even more rustic and were so faded that it was hard to distinguish the name of the pottery. Others were sparkling new and had clearly been made by professional sign makers. Their raised gold or green letters caught the eye and different graphic designs of purple pots or rainbow vases were a sharp contrast to the hand-painted letters wobbling across a board.

Molly studied her brochure on Seagrove, which she had borrowed from her mother before proposing the article to her editor. More than one hundred potteries were speckled over an area of about twenty-five miles. Though they were visited by busloads of tourists every year, it didn't seem possible that all of the potters could earn a living from the same trade. After all, Molly had never even heard of the area until her mother mentioned it, and she had lived in North Carolina for ten years.

Clara had informed her that many of the potters had full-time jobs. Some worked in the local mills or canneries, some raised livestock, and others worked as guest artists at schools around the state. Most of the potters were men. If they were married, their wives watched the "shop," which was often just a painted shed, while their husbands went to work. Over the weekends, the potters would turn and burn (an expression for creating pieces using the wheel then firing them in a kiln). Children of pottery families helped with the shop and if they showed the talent for it, began turning pieces or helping apply glaze at an early age.

This family lifestyle that centered on clay had been in place for over three hundred years in rural North Carolina.

Molly learned that most of the pottery was no longer made in the traditional way because very few potters could afford to pursue their craft on a full-time basis. Many now bought premixed clay and glazes to save time. Some potters even had commercial kilns, but most built their own, priding themselves on creating the vessel that would burn their wares. They often cut pine slabs from their own yards to feed the kiln's flames.

The potteries Clara drove by grew more and more spread out as they left the heart of Seagrove behind them. Some, like Jugtown Pottery, were down small lanes slightly off the beaten path, but these remote locations never hindered their success. For decades, hundreds of buyers and apprentices alike had traveled to seek the wares and knowledge of the family of potters who'd been in the same spot for generations.

Thin forests slowly gave way to pastures. Cows mingled lazily beneath the shade of ancient oak trees or slumped near the banks of small streams, searching for any available refuge from the heat. Both women were quiet in the car, conscious of the fact that they had both seen George-Bradley alive and well a few hours ago and now, in the space of a few heartbeats, he was dead.

"I feel sorry for him," Molly said, breaking the silence.

"Why?"

"Well, it seems to me that he was, you know, probably pretty lonely. And yes, one might say he deserved it for being a first-class jerk to most people, but is anyone going to miss him now that he's gone?"

Her mother shook her head. "I don't think so. That rude behavior at the kiln opening was so typical of George-Bradley. He was ungentlemanly and condescending to anyone he thought was a class below him. He even patronized the potters. Despite his behavior, he felt that his money and his incredible collection earned him a place of honor in everyone's eyes. Maybe he has family who will grieve, but I don't know a single person who will."

"Yet everyone knows his name. All of Randolph County knew who he was and everyone in the pottery circle did too. But no one will care. See, it's kind of sad."

"They'll care about his pottery, that's for sure. All the sharks will be circling around poor Bunny. People would kill to get their hands on George-Bradley's collection."

"And she hated it all, right? So won't she want to sell it?"

"You never know. She might want to hang on to the most valuable pieces for a while until the demand makes them worth even more money. She might want to give the whole collection to a museum. Then again, she might want to throw every piece against the wall. I don't know Bunny well. Like I said, she went her way and George-Bradley went his. Where that pottery is going to end up is a riddle I would love to be able to answer."

"Listen, Ma. I feel like there's something not quite right about his death. I didn't think to tell you this before, but he was acting really weird toward the end of the . . . the grabbing session." Molly described what she had witnessed behind the barn.

"Rubbing his stomach?" Clara was clearly perplexed. "I've heard of clutching your left arm during a heart attack, but this is a new one."

"Why would he go behind the barn to unbutton his shirt in the middle of a kiln opening? And why was he so out of it? It was like . . . I don't know, like he was drugged." The vision of George-Bradley's confused face nagged at her.

Clara pursed her lips. "Well, there certainly were plenty of people there who'd like to see him dead. Anyone who collects has to fight him off at every sale, but if it wasn't an accident, the police will know soon enough," she declared with finality.

"Maybe," Molly replied. Then because she didn't think her mother was taking her at all seriously, she added, "Or maybe I will. Knowing the complete truth is necessary if I want to write a killer article. George-Bradley is about to become more famous than he was before."

· · ·

Molly drove up to her little house feeling completely spent. Her cool, cozy rooms had never seemed so inviting. She sank down on her couch with a Diet Coke and some catalogues from her mail pile. Within seconds, a tan tabby hopped on her lap and began 'making biscuits,' as Molly liked to call it, by kneading her stomach with the claws of his front paws.

"Ow! Griffin! Here, have a nice pile of junk mail to sit on instead."

Molly made a pleasant nest of envelopes and Realtor advertisements for her cat. He happily relocated onto the pile and circled himself around until he was in prime bathing position.

"I swear, you are the vainest cat in all of Durham."

As Molly glanced over the glossy pages of Pottery Barn's fall collection, she felt her body slowly relaxing. Griffin's steady purring and the whir of the air conditioner soon sent her off to sleep.

The sound of the phone ringing jarred both her and the tabby into an upright position. They both blinked in surprise against the afternoon light but only Molly bothered to move from the sofa.

"Hello?" she croaked into the phone.

"Are you asleep when you should be in here typing up that article?" demanded the grating voice of her editor, Carl Swanson. He paused to take a drag from his cigarette. "I expect that piece on my desk by Monday!"

Carl was an overweight chain-smoker with a truculent nature and an obsession with the paper's circulation rate. The entire staff of *Collector's Weekly* lived in constant fear of Swanson's volatile temper and horrible breath, which was a blend of nicotine and strong black coffee.

"I was at the kiln opening at dawn," Molly said defensively. "I certainly got enough information for an article, but maybe a little more excitement than I'd bargained for. However"—she gave a theatrical pause—"this might be just the article to help our sales. A famous collector died today, Carl. But that's not all." She hesitated again, wondering if she was about to say something she would later regret, but the nagging feeling that followed her home from the kiln opening would not let go. "I don't think his death was accidental."

Molly could almost see her boss sitting up straighter in his chair, the ashes from his cigarette falling onto his expansive lap.

"Well? Go on, girlie! Give me all the details and let's see what we can print!"

Molly ignored his customary display of chauvinism and gave him a blow-by-blow account of the morning's events. Swanson was completely keyed up over the idea of publishing such a dramatic story.

"Get in here right away. I want you to go over the details with Matt Harrison."

Molly's heart skipped a beat. "Why Matt?"

"He went to med school at Duke. Didn't finish, but he's got some buddies in hospitals around here and we need those medical details to be accurate. Can't have you writing the wrong stuff and getting us sued."

Molly scowled at the implication that she wouldn't be able to acquire the correct information on her own and hung up on her boss as he began one of his lengthy coughing fits. Brightening at the thought of seeing Matt, Molly went upstairs to change her clothes. She wanted to look her best now that she'd finally be working with the man of her fantasies.

Twenty minutes later, Molly arrived at the paper's office building in northern Durham and made her way to the ladies' room, where she applied lipstick and ran a brush through her straight, dark hair.

Swanson must have briefed Matt, for he was waiting for her with his desk cleared, a welcoming smile on his face.

"I hadn't realized you went to medical school," she began.

A shadow crossed Matt's face. "For a little while, but I didn't finish. Listen," he said, hastening to change the subject, "why don't you tell me everything that happened this morning. Swanson's indicated that you believe this collector's death was suspicious. Is that true? Could you explain what you saw?"

Molly nodded, sensing a strong amount of doubt in Matt's voice. Still, she related her story once again, and he listened intently while occasionally jotting down notes on a legal pad. He was clearly more interested in the details of George-Bradley's demise than in the descriptions of the pottery or the behavior of the buyers after the rope was cut.

"So you heard that he had diabetes?"

"Yes, someone in line mentioned it after he was taken away in the ambulance," Molly said. "Or I might have heard it while he was stuffing his face with cookies. Either way, it seemed common knowledge."

Matt asked, "Did he look healthy?"

"No. He was overweight and sweating a lot. He kept dabbing at his face with a handkerchief. Plus, he was drinking tea and eating every sugary snack to be had like it was his last meal."

"Sweet tea?"

Molly laughed. "Boy, you give away that you're not from around here when you ask that. Of course it was sweet tea! Is there any other kind?"

Matt ignored her teasing. "It doesn't sound like he treated himself too well."

"Not in that regard." She proceeded to fill him in on the gossip about his affairs and his unusual marriage, pleased that she felt so comfortable talking to him. "The Stauntons," she concluded, "were a couple divided by his pottery collection. He put a great deal of time and energy into collecting. She hated everything he brought home."

"Well, I don't collect stuff, unless you count my beer bottle collection or my jar of wine corks. Does that mean I have to marry someone who likes beer bottles?"

Molly laughed. "I don't think that all married couples have that problem. After all, it's much more economical if only one person is spending money on eBay."

"I'm a cheapskate bachelor, so no problem there." He grinned and returned his attention to his legal pad.

A bachelor! Did he say that to let her know he was available? Molly tried to decipher the glimmer in Matt's light blue eyes but he was concentrating on his notes.

"Okay," he began, still looking at what he'd written. "I'm going to call in a favor from a friend over at Asheboro General. I'll find out the medical details. If there *is* something suspicious about this guy's death, and I'm not saying there is, medical science will bring it to light. Swanson wants this piece out on Monday, so why don't you start the article and I'll give you the filler you need by tonight? We could . . ." Molly watched as Matt stumbled for words and a ruddy blush crept up his cheeks.

"Order Chinese," she suggested quickly.

"Great." He smiled, and Molly returned to her desk and began typing up her article with a zippy rhythm.

• • •

By dinnertime, Molly was growing tired. Matt stopped by her desk as she was stifling a yawn.

"You'd better knock off for tonight," he said kindly. "We can go to that fondue restaurant next door. I'll write it off as a business expense."

"Yes, please. I can finish this up in the morning," she agreed gratefully.

After the waiter took their order for spicy cheese fondue, house salads, and an entrée of meat and seafood fondue, Matt seemed to grow fidgety. He crumpled and smoothed his napkin and glanced around the room, looking everywhere but at Molly.

"Did you talk to your friend at Asheboro General?" Molly asked, hoping to make him comfortable by sticking to work topics.

"Yes. Turns out that is the hospital where your collector was taken. My friend was doing his rotation in the ER when they brought him in, DOA."

Molly looked at him blankly. What did that acronyms mean? "DOA?"

Matt laughed. "Oh, sorry. It means Dead On Arrival."

"George-Bradley didn't even make it to the hospital?" Molly was surprised. So the customer at C.C.'s who'd said that an ambulance leaving without its sirens blaring meant the patient was already dead had been correct.

"No. And guess what his cause of death was?"

"I don't know. Heart attack?"

"No."

Molly thought about what else might have afflicted an overweight man. "Stroke?"

"No."

"Brain aneurysm?"

"Nope." Matt shook his head, his blue eyes smiling.

Molly lifted a skewered piece of bread dripping cheese onto her plate. Was Matt being playful with her? To test him, she replied in an exasperated voice, "Intensive probing by aliens?"

Matt raised his brows. "I'll give you a hint. It relates to the condition that you mentioned."

"Diabetes?"

"Yes."

"I don't know anything about diabetes, except that you have to take insulin, right?" Molly said.

"Right."

"So his death has something to do with insulin?"

Matt nodded. "Now you're getting warmer. Too much insulin, in fact."

"I don't get it."

"He died," Matt informed her proudly, "from an insulin overdose."

Molly stared at him. "An overdose? But don't people take insulin in pill form? Or injections? Can you give yourself too much? Explain, please."

"George-Bradley had Type Two diabetes. People with this condition produce some insulin, but not enough. Or the insulin they produce doesn't work right. You need a certain amount of glucose to keep your body running. Insulin gets the glucose into your cells. Following me so far?"

"Yes, and thank you for putting this into layman's terms for me."

Matt took a breath and continued. "Usually, people who have Type Two diabetes are middle-aged and overweight. Their cells can't absorb glucose because they don't have enough insulin to let the glucose in, so it's kind of hanging around in their bloodstream. Lots of people with Type Two can control this by following a careful diet and exercising on a regular basis."

"Something George-Bradley didn't do. He was clearly out of

shape, and when I saw him at the kiln opening, he was smoking too. He totally reeked of tobacco."

"And since he didn't maintain a healthy lifestyle, he needed to take insulin shots to regulate his glucose levels. Considering he was an overweight smoker, it's amazing he didn't have problems before this."

"How do people know how much insulin to take?" Molly asked.

"They have portable instruments that measure their blood glucose, or blood sugar levels, as most people say, then they know if it's time for a dose. Most diabetics can sense when they're in need of insulin. They start feeling weak or dizzy. Some people give themselves shots at regular intervals, like before breakfast and dinner. But diabetes patients can be really different, and there are several different types of insulin. It really depends upon the individual."

"What happens if you get an overdose of insulin?"

"That's called hypoglycemia. Too much insulin makes the body lose its sugar, or its energy. George-Bradley's body just shut down. He was probably comatose before the ambulance even left the garage."

"But I still don't understand. If he gave himself regular shots, how could he give himself too much?"

Matt shrugged. "It's not common, but I guess he could have forgotten that he already had a shot or misread his blood glucose level. By the time that rope was cut, his adrenaline was pumping, he had eaten a bunch of sugary foods, and he had taken a double dose of insulin to boot. I don't know how it happened. All I know is that it was a mistake that cost him his life."

"Wow." Molly tried to absorb all of the medical details. "That's awful. Did you find out anything else?"

"I didn't really ask. I mean all this stuff is confidential, remember? And all you can put in your article is what has been officially released to the press, which isn't much."

"It's a start." Molly thought for a moment. "But his cause of death will be made known to his wife and the insurance company, right?"

"Yes, why?"

Molly wiped the condensation off the surface of her water glass as an idea struck her. "What if the insurance company views George-Bradley's death as a suicide?"

"Did he seem like someone on the verge of committing suicide?"

"Not at all! He was in his element, according to my mother, and when I met him, he was as pleased as a pig in mud." Molly hesitated, recalling the image of George-Bradley staggering off behind the barn. "The last time I saw him, he was acting dazed, confused. He was rubbing this spot of skin on his stomach. Something was completely wrong about the way he was moving, too. If he had given himself an extra dose, why would he look so surprised about a sore patch of skin?" Molly paused, remembering another detail. "I think I remember a tiny bloodstain on his shirt too. What could that mean?"

Matt dunked a piece of lobster in a bowl of seasoned butter and shrugged. "Sounds like he was examining the place where he gave himself his last injection. Did you see a syringe?"

"No, but I know he didn't kill himself. He was definitely not the type. He was having the time of his life. There was nothing but anticipation in his eyes until that moment behind the barn. Something else happened at that kiln opening. Something that caused George-Bradley's death. I'm certain of it."

"In that case, I doubt anyone else will think it's a suicide either." Matt paused, not wanting to offend her. "I'm sure everyone will think that his death was a thoughtless accident. Just a stupid but fatal mistake."

• • •

Molly thanked Matt for dinner and they parted in the parking deck. She had hoped he would ask to see her again, but then she remembered that they hadn't been on a date, just a working dinner. Tired to the bone, she drove home and phoned her best friend Kitty before turning in for the night.

Kitty and Molly had once taught together at the same private school. To earn extra money, Molly used to help out at Lex Lewis's antique sales, serving as a runner, a clerk, or as floor manager. During an important quarterly sale, Lex had needed another person to help with registration and checkout and Molly had brought Kitty along. Sparks flew the moment Lex and Kitty met, and now they were married and living a few streets away from Clara. They were known in Hillsborough as the town's most outwardly affectionate couple. At any given time, one could witness what Clara called "one of their nauseating displays of kissing and pet name calling."

"Chicken!" Kitty screeched the nickname she had given Molly years ago. "What's going on?"

"Girl, you have no idea." And Molly told the story yet again. Kitty wanted to hear every detail, down to what Clara and Molly had eaten for brunch. Because Kitty saw many of the collectors at Lex's auctions, she knew some of the names Molly mentioned.

"That George-Bradley was a regular louse!" she exclaimed, then lowered her voice. "I tell you, every time he came over to my desk to checkout after a sale he would just stare at my chest. No shame at all—just stare, stare, stare. I couldn't stand the man!"

"You don't seem to be alone there. The good news is, I got to discuss the whole event with Matt over dinner."

"*The* Matt? Oh, *do* tell."

"It was just a working dinner, nothing romantic. Still, we got along well together, I think. I certainly enjoyed it."

"Did you talk about anything personal? Like whether or not he has a girlfriend?"

Molly hesitated. "He's not married, but I don't know if he's dating anyone. I did learn that he almost finished med school but . . ."

"But what?"

"I don't know. I got the feeling that it wasn't a safe subject to discuss. Obviously he dropped out for a reason, and I didn't think I should pry."

"Maybe not about that, but you'd better talk to that boy. Now that you've had dinner, the door is open for all kinds of possibilities!" Kitty trilled.

"Oh, do I wish. He's smart, hardworking, and mighty easy on the eye. Anyway, I've got to listen to a message from my editor before I pass out from exhaustion so I'll talk to you tomorrow."

"I can't wait to tell Lex about the kiln opening. You know he and your mom will be aching to get their hands on George-Bradley's pottery. Sweet dreams of Matt," Kitty said and hung up.

Molly reluctantly listened to the rough voice of Carl Swanson growl through the speaker of her answering machine.

"I have another collector for you to see. Hope you've got a pencil," he said, his voice convulsing into a cough. "We're going to print a series on Asheboro collectors. Kind of 'the prime cache of pottery in the middle of the state' theme. Once you're done with the George-Bradley piece, go see a man named Hillary Keane. Yeah, I know, what kind of man's name is Hillary? Must be a sissy. I'll e-mail you his number and address. According to my sources, this guy has an incredible collection. I called him to see if he'd be willing to do the interview, and it's set up for Tuesday at noon. Find out how he got started, where he buys, and photograph his best pieces. We want lots of pictures and he hates having his stuff photographed, so wear something pretty and kiss his butt a little, whatever it takes."

Great. There's nothing I like better than a hostile interviewee, thought Molly as Swanson's voice ceased. She'd had experience with men and women like Keane, snobs who wanted to brag about their collection and yet didn't want anyone to know too many specifics. On the other hand, Keane had been at the kiln opening and George-Bradley had cut in front of him in line. Perhaps this was her chance to begin her detective work.

Molly looked around at her pile of unread mail and sighed. She usually took Sundays and Tuesdays off as she worked Saturdays, but she could see that arguing with Swanson would get her nowhere in view of his current circulation obsession.

A furry body rubbed against her leg, then trotted off toward the kitchen of Molly's tiny house. She followed the darting shadow in time to see Griffin jump up to a sitting position on the inside of the dishwasher door. His eyes were large and expectant.

"You need a treat, I suppose."

The coddled feline meowed in agreement.

Rummaging in the fridge, she pulled out a can of whipped topping and made a rippled cream heart on the dishwasher lid. Griffin happily lapped at her design. Molly stared at the flimsy heart and thought of Matt. She wondered if their dinner together had caused her name to cross his mind as he settled in for the night. And though she expected to dream of him, she fell into a deep sleep filled with visions of the wicked grins of pottery face jugs.

Chapter 5

I say, you look upon this verse,
When I perhaps compounded am with clay,
Do not so much as my poor name rehearse,
But let your love even with my life decay.
  —William Shakespeare, Sonnet LXXI

T he coffee maker gurgled and bubbled as the aroma of French vanilla filled the little kitchen. The television was set to the Weather Channel, and Molly missed the local forecast for the third time as she responded to a chorus of cat cries. As she was popping two blueberry waffles in the toaster, the phone rang. Molly knew that a call at this time of the morning could only be from one of three people: her mother, grandmother, or Kitty. She examined her caller ID. It was Clara.

"'Morning, Ma."

"How did you know it was me? Oh, that's right, you've got that ID thing . . . Listen, I have *very* exciting news."

Molly knew from the way her mother's voice dropped to a stage whisper that this news had something to do with antiques or pottery and that it was *big*.

"Guess who called me this morning?"

"Grandma," Molly guessed.

"Yes, but guess who else," Clara demanded impatiently.

"Lex."

"Yes!" Clara exclaimed. "And guess who called *him*?"

Molly paused. Who could have sent auctioneer Lex Lewis and her mother into a complete tizzy? After closing her antiques shop, Clara started working part-time at Lex's auction gallery in Hillsborough. Months later, Lex found he couldn't survive without her and Clara became a silent partner. Though she still ran her own pottery business,

Clara found she couldn't bear to sell any of the rare pieces she'd acquired. Her house became more and more crowded and her "shop" remained rather thin in the inventory department. She put pieces on her website every now and then for good measure.

At the auction company, Clara set her own schedule and salary. She often used her flexible workday to drum up interest in Lex's pottery sales. Clara had a good eye for what was saleable and often accompanied Lex when he viewed estate sales or a private collection.

Judging by her mother's exuberant tone, a well-known collector must have called Lex to look over his or her goods. Whose house would Clara love to be invited to visit?

"Was it Bunny Staunton?"

"You got it, Madam!" Her mother was bursting at the seams with anticipation. "The funeral is scheduled for Monday, and she already left a message on the auction gallery's answering machine early this morning asking Lex to drive right out to Asheboro and look at the collection."

"The funeral is scheduled for Monday? As in day after tomorrow?"

"Yes."

"And she wants you guys over there today? Isn't this all a bit sudden?" Molly asked incredulously. Funerals were a big thing in the South. And if George-Bradley's body was being released, then the police must not consider his death suspicious.

Molly could sense her mother shrugging over the phone. Clara was too busy fantasizing about pottery to worry about Bunny's motives. Impatiently she replied, "Oh, Bunny must be dying to get rid of that pottery. She's always hated the stuff. Get over here this minute! We're leaving at eleven and you don't want to miss it."

Her mother's excitement was contagious. Molly was going to have the chance to see one of the finest collections in the region, intact, before it was sent to auction and the feeding frenzy began.

"No, I don't want to miss it," she assured her mother. "Be right over."

• • •

Kitty waited out in the driveway of Clara's house. A traditional North Carolina "shotgun" home, the decrepit structure was on the list of endangered houses when Clara spotted it in her Preservation Society magazine. At the time, she was living in a cookie-cutter neighborhood, where every third house was exactly the same except for the hue of the vinyl siding. The builder had cut corners wherever possible. The house had looked fine from the outside, but little details like cheap light fixtures, sparse landscaping, and the lack of wainscotings made Clara long for a residence with more character.

When she read that an 1830s farmhouse was soon to be torched as practice for the local fire department, she hopped in the car and drove out to the site. With her ability to envision the potential in things, Clara knew that her desire for a house with personality was about to be fulfilled. She bought the house and its three outbuildings for a total of $1,500.

Of course, it cost many times that amount to move it to its new lot. Builders had to load the structure in two halves on the beds of two tractor-trailers in order to deliver it to Hillsborough.

The chimney was also disassembled and reassembled brick by brick, and the log cabin outbuilding rebuilt by a pricey expert.

Surrounded by perennial gardens, tulip poplars, and crepe myrtles, the house looked like it had always belonged on the gentle rise where it peered down upon a quiet street. At the time, Molly thought her mother had gone completely mad. Who would deliberately embark on such a complicated and risky project? But once the house was rebuilt, Molly was proud that Clara had saved a piece of history and had restored the farmer's home to its simple beauty. It was doubtful, however, that the original owners had as many cats as Clara.

Kitty was stroking the fur of one of them. The happy creature was named Arthur Ray Cole after one of the area potters. He was a lean, glossy, black cat who rolled on his back with pleasure as Kitty scratched under his chin. Tall and stick thin, Kitty had a cloud of dark, curly brown hair and wide blue eyes, as pale as the moonlit snow. When she heard Molly's car, she stood up and waved.

"Hey, Chicken!" she greeted her friend in her high, light voice. "Ready to see some stuff?"

"Absolutely. I have my camera too, in case Bunny lets me take some pictures for a future article."

"Lex and your mom are beside themselves. I think we need two bibs for the drooling."

Molly laughed. "Tell me about the message Bunny left."

"It was pretty short and to the point. She said that she heard that Lex had handled the deaccession sale for the Mint Museum"—and here Kitty broke out into a very exaggerated drawl and mimicked Bunny's voice—"and I may not know much about *pottery*, but I *do* know *people*. Several of my good friends are board members for the museum, so you come *highly* recommended."

"Wow. So then Lex called her back and she wanted him over lickety-split?" Molly asked.

"She's going to redecorate," announced Lex, hopping down the porch stairs in front of Clara. Lex was a bit shorter than Kitty, with close-cropped brown hair and a neat, light brown beard. His chestnut eyes were bright with anticipation. "Right, darling?" He grabbed one of Kitty's hands and planted a kiss on her freckled skin.

"Enough yapping!" Clara quickly clapped her hands and ordered everyone into Lex's van. "Time to go. Hurry, hurry, hurry!"

• • •

The Staunton residence was just south of Asheboro, an easy commute to George-Bradley's law office in the business district. Driving through the town, it was obvious that the year's drought and bad economy had left their mark on the local businesses. Many of the storefronts were vacant. For Lease or For Rent signs hung in every third window. Most of the stores in operation had large red sale signs in their windows, but the attempts to attract customers did not seem to be working.

The streets were nearly empty. A few people meandered on the sidewalks or looked in windows, but it was very quiet for a Saturday morning in June. The block where George-Bradley's law office was located was tucked away down a side street, but Molly caught the gilt lettering of his sign as the van passed by.

"What do you think will happen to his practice?" she asked out loud.

"He's got a partner," her mother replied, "so I'm sure it will continue under a different name."

Molly mused over the gilt sign. It would soon be replaced and George-Bradley's lengthy name would be missing from the new gilt plaque. It would also be erased from the office's letterhead, business cards, legal documents, and slowly, from memory. It was a sobering thought.

Heading south, Lex drove just outside the city limits and turned right onto a curved lane lined with ancient magnolia trees. They were in bloom; their wide, creamy flowers sat like cupped hands in the waxy leaves. The thick branches met and intertwined across the heights of the narrow lane, creating a sun-speckled path to the Staunton Estate.

At the foot of the driveway, two stately wrought iron gates had been opened wide for their arrival, controlled electronically from the house. A beautiful cobblestone driveway, slick with water after a morning wash, led them up a crested hill dotted with dogwoods, pear trees, and crepe myrtles. Each side of the driveway was lined with a bed of lilies, coneflowers, and black-eyed Susans. There wasn't so much as a leaf out of place in the yard. When the house came into view, Molly gasped.

A large Georgian brick, the house greeted them with a wide front veranda bordered by boxwood bushes. Thick white columns flanked the door and a flagstone path wove off to the side, leading to a walled kitchen garden. From the center of the house, two long wings stretched off symmetrically to each side, giving the impression of a pair of strong arms resting on the ground. The beige trim was clean, the black shutters shone as if newly painted, the windows sparkled without streaks in the morning sun, and the front step welcomed them with a woven doormat with the letter *S* monogrammed upon it.

Lex moved forward and rang the bell. A series of ding-dongs purred through the house. Molly half expected a butler to answer the door, stiff-necked and dressed in full house uniform, but Bunny opened it, releasing a cloud of perfume into the morning air.

Bunny looked much like the other wealthy Southern women who came to Lex's auctions. She was short and round with plump arms and sausage-shaped fingers. She wore a long black pantsuit with a chartreuse linen shirt-jacket on top. A thick collar of gold fit snugly around her neck, and she wore several gold bracelets, a Rolex, and rings with large stones on each hand. Her right hand bore a large emerald and her left, a yellow diamond. Her hair was dyed a white blonde that had lost any true sense of color and was curled until it formed a puffed bob. Molly instinctively knew that it was also disciplined into its form with enough hairspray to choke a bull.

Bunny's face was a mask of makeup including green eye shadow and mauve lipstick. It had been deftly applied and made to look subtle, but in combination with the jewels, the hair, and the strong, musky perfume, Bunny gave the impression that she was just on her way to a high couture fashion show. She hardly looked like a widow mourning the loss of her husband. And the expression on her face was all business. Without smiling, she stepped back from the doorframe, allowing them inside. She arched a thin, drawn eyebrow over seeing four people enter when she had only telephoned one.

Lex made the introductions, explaining that his three "assistants" would help him write descriptions of all the objects Bunny was interested in selling. That would enable him to give Bunny a more accurate quote for the auction contract.

Bunny waved his explanation off with an impatient flick of her hand. "I don't need a quote. You're the man for this job, and I'm not concerned about what you get for this stuff, I just want it out of the house."

Her voice was low and humorless. Molly wondered how she was coping with her husband's death. He was a man with whom she seemed to have shared a passionless marriage. Was it a loveless one as well? George-Bradley had cheated on her, filled the house with things she disliked, and avoided her presence. Though Bunny did not look the part of the grieving widow, Molly had a feeling that she was an expert at concealing her feelings. Were there traces of tension and pain beneath the flat voice and the immovable face?

"Ma'am?" Molly asked sweetly, already planning ahead for an article on the Stauntons. "Do you mind if I photograph the items you want to sell?"

"Not at all. You'll need pictures for the auction anyway, won't you? As far as I'm concerned, you can box it all and get it out of here today."

Lex was unprepared for this. Typically, he went into a residence, looked over the items, and then discussed with the owner the probable value, when it would be sold, and what he would charge for his commission. If accepted, he and the other party would sign a contract and Lex would pack up all of the items to move them to a storage space. If Bunny was offering him items without reviewing the contract right away, they must only be the low-end or damaged pieces from George-Bradley's collection.

"Let's see how much we're talking about." Lex couldn't hide his disappointment. If Bunny was only selling a few pieces of chipped pottery, they had all gotten excited for nothing.

"All of it, naturally. I am going to completely redecorate this wing of the house"—Bunny gestured grandly—"so all four rooms in my . . ." She paused. "That were George-Bradley's can be cleared out."

"Including furniture?" Lex's good humor was instantly restored.

"Everything," Bunny said firmly. "Down to the last paper clip in his desk. I don't want a single item left there, is that understood?"

The four friends were silent. Bunny could not have made it more evident how she felt about her husband. She had hated him. She was getting rid of all signs of his presence, and she was wasting no time about it.

"I understand, and I can take care of everything for you," Lex assured her, which was the perfect reply.

"I'll leave you to it then." She nodded her head in dismissal and crossed the hall to the other wing, which had been her domain in the divided house.

Clara wisely closed the door leading into the hall, so that the four of them could react to their discoveries without being overheard.

"Wow!" Clara grabbed onto Lex's arm and gave him a shake. "Did you hear what she said?"

"I did!" Lex replied gleefully. "I heard the word *everything*."

The cause for their excitement was obvious, because this room contained valuable antiques, the most eye-catching of them being a large grandfather clock with a paint-decorated face.

"Walnut," Lex informed them.

"Looks Virginia-made," Clara said as she peered into the face. "Early. It's right too."

She and Lex exchanged happy looks. Whenever one of them said, "It's right," what they meant was, "This is a real antique that has not been damaged or refinished and it will bring a lot of money at auction." But Molly knew it was more than that. Lex and Clara respected a good antique piece. They were harder and harder to find these days, so it was a joy to see something so pristine and graceful, an object of history created by means of a true craftsman's passion and hard work.

Clara had once told Molly that a person could really fall in love with a chest of drawers, a quilt, or a piece of pottery.

Molly understood. It was the power of owning something made by hand. These pieces possessed a kind of magic. It was the mark left inside the grain of wood, the strings of thread, or the smooth skin of clay. It held there, fast, through the decades, yet only certain people felt its presence.

Kitty, impatient to get an overview of the rooms, had gone ahead. Now she ran back into the front room, her eyes round with wonder.

"You guys are going to pass out!" She pointed down the hall.

But Lex and Clara would not be tempted beyond the living room. They had an 1840s sugar chest to look over, a collection of Chinese import porcelain to view, the weave on an Oriental carpet to examine, and several old oil paintings in gilt frames to inspect. Molly took the bait, however, and followed Kitty's bouncing steps down the corridor.

The first room must have been George-Bradley's office. His large, leather-topped desk was the only piece of furniture in the room other than the rows of bookshelves. The shelves covered every open wall and partially obscured both windows. Each one held three to seven pieces of pottery. The shelves were perfectly dusted and labeled with a little card that identified the pottery, the maker, and the year purchased. George-Bradley's desk was stacked with a neat pile of reference books on pottery as well as general price guides and books on collecting antiques. Except for last week's Sunday paper, there were no loose papers on the desk surface. George-Bradley clearly liked organization.

Molly looked over the pottery quickly as Kitty was calling her again from the next room. According to the labels, the same potter made most of the pieces, a man named Ben Owen. Molly had heard of him only because her mother had a few of his vases on her dining room mantel. She also knew that his work was strongly influenced by Asian shapes and glazes, and that he made several exquisite vases each year that sold for around two thousand dollars apiece.

George-Bradley had six of these, standing in a dignified row on two bottom shelves. The glaze was called "Chinese blue," even though it was mostly red in tone with some hints of blue that peeked through in a brilliant shade reminiscent of the Mediterranean Sea.

Clara and Lex appeared in the office.

"My heavens," her mother breathed. "I have never seen this much Ben Owen in one room."

"Look at these Han vases!" Lex exclaimed. "They're perfect. Think of what an awesome catalogue cover they'd make!"

Clara and Lex were in their element. They showed each other piece after piece, admiring the shape, the shimmers of glaze, and the complete lack of chips or firing cracks.

"He certainly had excellent taste," her mother complimented George-Bradley. "There isn't a piece in here that doesn't catch your eye and demand further inspection and admiration."

Molly left Clara and Lex to salivate and continued on to where Kitty waited in the sitting room across the hall. It had a small leather couch and matching wingback chairs turned toward the fireplace. Oriental throw rugs warmed the room in red and blue tones, while English hunting prints raced along the wood-paneled walls. On top of a small hunt board, crystal decanters with sterling silver labels indicated that while gin and vodka were available, the favorite drink was clearly bourbon.

A set of shelves was built into the back wall only. The other walls were given space for a cherry game table and two very old Southern stands. Both of the stands held stacks of small, leather-bound books and a collection of carriage clocks, which ticked merrily away as Molly examined the pottery.

"Isn't this your favorite potter?" Kitty asked, holding the figure of a lion out toward Molly.

"Billy Ray Hussey. Yes, it is. I only have one piece, though. Mom gave me one of his cat doorstops for my birthday." She took the lion from Kitty and examined him with wonder. His solid body was glazed a burnt yellow, like the underside of a sunflower petal. His large brown mane was made from dozens and dozens of individual curls of clay, and his red roaring mouth sported a row of white teeth.

"Look at that mane." Kitty admired the curls while patting her own. "Kind of looks like mine."

"I read that they call that fur 'Cole slaw' in the pottery world. All those little pieces of clay."

"Are you saying that my hair looks like slaw?" Kitty asked, pretending to be insulted.

Molly smiled, and then pointed to the figure of a poodle with tons of curled clay fired in a white glaze. Kitty showed her a shelf of silly, smiling face jugs, and the women touched the chips of broken dishes that formed the rows of teeth.

"Shall we proceed?" she asked Kitty.

Except for the bathroom, the final room in George-Bradley's wing was a large sunroom with windows overlooking three different views. Walking over to the sparkling glass, Molly was granted a view of an immaculately landscaped pool complete with outdoor bar and tables with umbrellas. Beyond the pool she could make out a tennis court nestled in a grove of mature oaks.

"Bunny must've come with a *lot* of money," Kitty observed, in a loud, singsong voice.

"Kitty!" Molly scolded. "Hush!"

The windows directly in front of them overlooked the slope of green lawn leading down to the drive. A gardener was busy weeding one of the beds. His broad back faced the windows, and though Molly couldn't see his face, his muscular arms and baseball cap gave the impression of both strength and youth.

The furniture in this room was simple. There was a long pine church pew running beneath the windows along the longest wall, an antique music stand, and some kind of wooden box on a side table. Molly moved toward the box and gingerly lifted the lid.

"Kitty, look."

The women stared down at an old windup music box. Beneath a glass window, five brass bells waited to be rung out by five silver birds whose beaks would delicately peck at them, creating an accompaniment to the song played by the rolling cylinder dotted with raised notes.

"Do we dare?" Molly asked, gazing in wonder at the tiny birds.

"We do," Kitty answered and carefully pulled up the crank that would wind the box.

"Just crank it one or two times, so we can hear a few notes. We don't know how loud it's going to be."

As they watched the cylinder begin to move, the women held their breaths. The music began. It was like nothing Molly had ever heard. Sweet notes like trickling water tripped along with the resonating chimes of the birds striking the bells. The sound was light and high, yet reverberated within the depths of the wooden box, creating an echo. It was the music of fantasy, of rain falling on the pond's skin, of a butterfly bursting from its chrysalis in silence of the night. It was the hypnotizing language of fairies, of dragonflies.

Lex and Clara couldn't deny the pull of the music, and the four stood like statues as it moved through them. Molly looked above the box and saw that several old instruments hung from the walls. There was a trumpet, a clarinet, and a flute. On the opposite wall hung a banjo, a tambourine, and a violin.

When the music stopped Kitty whispered in awe, "For such an unpleasant person, he sure had some wonderful things."

"Professor Plum, with the wrench, in the Music Room," Lex joked to lift the serious mood, his gaze falling upon the old instruments. No one got his joke. "Clue?" he said. "Remember the board game? Oh, forget it."

Undeterred, Clara explained that the shelves covering the back wall were divided into two sections. One half contained the pottery of Jack Graham and face jugs and churns by C.C. Burle. The second set contained fragile roosters by a Georgia family of potters called the Meaders and ovoid jugs from Edgefield, South Carolina.

Encased in glass, one large jug stood aside from the others.

"What's this?" Molly asked her mother.

"That, my dear, is a piece of pottery created by a black man known as Dave the Slave. It's only worth about twenty thousand dollars!"

"Wow," she said, picking up an Edgefield crock. "What are these orange stickers on the bottom of each one?"

"Looks like inventory stickers. He must have a master list stored somewhere around here," Clara said.

Molly moved over to the shelves containing Jack Graham's pottery. She immediately loved his work. His vases were small and elegant, fired in crimson reds and deep blues. There were also large vases with wider mouths and fluted rims. Some were swirled in browns and coppery yellows, but others were glazed a cobalt blue and covered with white or yellow drippings. He made large bowls with glazed snakes inside, spiraled and dotted with red curly tongues. Molly reached up and drew down a blue vase with wide shoulders that rose up to a thin, graceful neck.

"Mom," she breathed, "his work is amazing."

Clara watched her daughter's eyes glow in wonder, turning over the vase she held.

"There's nothing like it—to fall in love with something another person loved to create."

"I can sense it," Molly said softly, feeling a little embarrassed. "I can tell what he put into this piece. It's like his hands are still moving over it."

"I told you," Clara said triumphantly. "Once you've got the bug, you can't go back. Kiss all of your money and your sanity good-bye! Lex, I think you'll have a new bidder at your next sale."

Molly turned the vase upside down and a small piece of paper fluttered to the ground.

"Looks like a portion of a newspaper article." Molly stooped to retrieve the scrap. "It's been highlighted."

"What does it say?" Clara craned her neck over her daughter's shoulder as Molly proffered the article. It read:

E.M.—Now, I know you don't make human figurals, but how about animals?

J.G.—No. I stick to pieces I can make by turning.

E.M.—Do you ever think you'll make a figural in the future? How about an experimental cat or a horse?

J.G.—No, I'll leave those for the more talented potters out there. I just never had the notion to make anything off the wheel.

E.M.—Well, if you ever made one I'm sure it would be exceptionally valuable.

"E.M. must be the interviewer and J.G. must be Jack Graham," Molly said. "I wonder why George-Bradley kept this." She then began to examine the bottom of the vase she held. Jack Graham had signed his initials instead of using a metal stamp like most of the other potters. He had also scraped a number into the unglazed clay.

"What's this number?" she asked her mother.

Clara took the vase from her hands. "That's the kiln number. There are fifty to seventy-five pieces of pottery that survive each kiln load. This is an early one. He made this piece, put the number in the clay, and fired the kiln for the fifth time."

"Fifth time ever?" Molly wondered how long ago that was.

Clara nodded. "Yes, from the time he began numbering pieces. I think he made a few kiln loads without numbers first, before he really began selling as a full-time potter. He started off as a welder."

"And he quit his job to make pottery? Did he have any experience?"

"No, he just loved it. It didn't run in his family like it did for most of the other potters. He just tried using the wheel one day and knew he had to learn. Remember what C.C. said, that he had to make pots whether people bought them or not."

Kitty stood over the music stand and thumbed through the large black book that had been resting on its polished surface.

"Hey, guys, I think this is the inventory book." She offered it to Lex.

Lex looked over the book's contents. "Okay," he said, holding it out to them decisively, "first thing we do is make sure all these pieces match with the descriptions recorded in this book. George-Bradley has added details about every piece down to what riverbed the clay came from, so we already have a great start for the catalogue descriptions."

"When will we pack this up?" Kitty asked.

"We only have a couple boxes in the van. I wasn't prepared to pack today. I'll come back on Monday with the big truck and some guys to get it all at once."

"Let's start in the office and work our way back," Clara suggested.

As Lex read from the inventory list, the three women located the pottery and he checked each one off with a pencil.

"Number 3124. A Ben Owen ovoid vase in red glaze."

It should have been easy to find the pottery. The ware was grouped together by maker, the shelves were labeled, and each bore an orange inventory sticker.

"Not here," Clara said, reexamining the shelves. "Maybe he has some upstairs."

"Maybe it's mixed in with some of the other pieces in the other rooms," Kitty offered doubtfully, checking again on the bottom shelves.

After looking through two rooms, including closets, the group discovered that three pieces were missing from George-Bradley's collection.

"Onto the music room," Lex directed.

Checking off from the list, Lex announced that a small Meaders rooster, a Jugtown teapot, and a Northstate vase were missing. That made six pieces in total from the mixed collection.

"Didn't Bunny say all of George-Bradley's saleable items were in this wing?" Clara asked.

"That's what I understood," said Lex.

Molly reviewed the descriptions of the pottery from the inventory book. "They're all smaller pieces," she noticed.

"Maybe they're getting repaired," Kitty suggested.

"George-Bradley was very particular about his pottery," Clara dismissed the notion. "He'd never need to have a piece repaired. He only bought pieces in mint condition."

"Unless the cleaning lady chipped them," Kitty persisted.

"I think George-Bradley took care of cleaning the shelves himself." Lex pointed to a feather duster hanging from a hook on the side of one of the shelves. "Those six pieces have to be somewhere else in the house. When we're done with the Jack Grahams, I'll ask Bunny."

The Jack Graham collection was as orderly as the rest. George-Bradley had one or two pieces from every firing from number one to number forty-two. That piece was a long-necked pitcher called a Rebecca pitcher. The next piece, number forty-four, was a simple brown shoulder vase, probably the only piece in the collection that seemed to lack personality. Piece number forty-five was identical.

"Where's number forty-three?" Kitty asked.

Lex frowned over the book. "He doesn't have it written down."

"He has every kiln number but that one?" Clara was surprised.

"Must have missed that sale." Lex shrugged. "Let's write a quick list of the furniture and then head out."

"Good, I'm starving," Kitty whined. Lex put his arm around her waist and gave it a squeeze. As he began whispering endearments in his wife's ear, Clara cleared her throat loudly.

Unabashed, Lex gave Kitty a kiss on the check and declared, "Lunch is on me, ladies. We'll have one of our IHOP specials."

Dreaming of crepes and bacon, cheeseburgers and fries dipped in ranch dressing, and huge glasses of sweet tea, the foursome got back to work.

They finished taking inventory quickly, driven by hunger and Lex's anxiety to return to the auction gallery to pick a date for what would likely be one of his finest sales.

"Let me find Bunny to tell her we're done for today."

"Don't forget to ask about the six pieces of missing pottery, sweetie," Kitty reminded her husband, blowing kisses at him.

"Oh, I won't, sugar pie," he said sweetly.

Clara rolled her eyes in disgust.

Back in the main hall, the group listened for any stirrings in the rest of the house. The door to Bunny's wing was slightly ajar, so Lex pushed on it while giving a cautionary tap.

"Mrs. Staunton? Ma'am?"

He knocked a little louder. The sounds of a woman's voice floated out to them. Bunny spoke, and then there was a pause, then she spoke again.

"She must be on the phone," Molly deduced. "I'll just poke my head in and give her the hand sign that we're leaving."

No one else wanted to go, so her offer was readily accepted. Truth be told, Molly just wanted a peek of the other half of the house, knowing she wouldn't be back for Lex's subsequent visits.

She entered the spacious living room, wincing at the bright yellow wallpaper and heavy flowered curtains, getting a glimpse of two plush green chairs facing a yellow-striped sofa strewn with embroidered pillows in yellows, pinks, and greens.

The overdose of color propelled her forward into the hall, but not before she noticed the wedding portrait over the mantel. It was Bunny and George-Bradley, radiant with happiness and expectation. Bunny was gazing at her new husband with a look of pure adoration, a look that Molly had trouble imagining on the present Bunny's face. There were also a dozen photographs lining the mantel. They were all of a happy Staunton couple, taken over a space of twenty years.

Bunny's voice was coming from the furthest room, the one mirroring George-Bradley's music room. Before Molly could announce her presence, Bunny's angry words cut through the air.

"But that is *simply* ridiculous!" she yelled in frustration, emphasizing every word. "I told you, he took his insulin *every morning before breakfast*. He took it that morning and I would know because I gave it to him!" There was a pause as the caller spoke. "He would fill the syringe and hand it to me. No, I don't know how much was in it. I never looked."

This was followed by another pause as Bunny listened to the reply. Molly didn't know where to turn. Her feet were rooted to the ground, curiosity overcoming good manners.

"Look, my husband was very predictable. First the shot, then some coffee, a glass of freshly squeezed orange juice, three eggs over easy, and four pieces of bacon. Every morning for ten years. He hated giving himself the shot and I certainly didn't mind giving it to him. After all, I am his wife," Bunny added in a defensive tone.

Bunny paused again, sighing in annoyance.

"Well, that may be the case, but I'm telling you, he had his morning shot at home!"

Molly heard Bunny slam down the receiver in anger. "Why don't you ask me if I'm glad that my husband had diabetes?" Bunny raged aloud in her office, unaware that she had an audience on the other side of the door. "Why don't you ask me if I'm glad that he's dead?"

Molly backed quietly out of the hall. Once she was standing in the yellow living room she coughed loudly.

"Mrs. Staunton?" she called innocently, walking back into the hallway.

Bunny poked her head out of the office door, a manila envelope held protectively to her chest.

"I'm sorry to interrupt you, but I just wanted to let you know that there are a few pieces of pottery listed in your husband's inventory book that aren't on the shelves." Molly talked faster as Bunny stared at her in disinterest. "Could they be anywhere else in the house?"

"No. All of his pottery is in that wing."

Molly shifted from one foot to another. "Do you have a cleaning service?"

Bunny frowned. "We do. Two wonderful ladies who've been cleaning for us for years. If they broke anything, they'd tell me immediately. I have complete trust in them."

The phone in the office began to ring again. Bunny scowled. "They were probably taken by some of his *collector* friends. They were always dropping by to see his collection, whether he was here or not." She began to turn away, and then paused and added, "And what did I care? I let them in. Now, if you'll excuse me." Bunny returned to the safety of her office and shut the door before Molly could ask her the names of these "friends."

Back in the main hall, Lex cocked an eyebrow at her. "You're making a funny face. What did she say?"

"I'll tell you in the car," Molly said, relieved that they were leaving.

The Staunton house might be beautiful, but there were some dark corners in the polished mansion where mysteries lurked. Why would a woman who hated her husband keep so many pictures of him near her? Had George-Bradley received his daily insulin shot and then absentmindedly given himself another one? Or had Bunny deliberately given her philandering husband an overdose? And where, in a house that guarded its secrecy beneath a façade of expensive decorators and immaculate landscaping, were the missing pieces of pottery?

• • •

The hands that held the rabbit were not gentle. They were smooth and oily, missing the calluses of work and the coarseness that comes with creation. They were damp, greedy hands that put too much pressure on the clay's hollow neck. Strange smells that were not of the earth, but spoke of dead trees and ink, seeped into the clay's pores, and it protested as the crush of an old piece of newspaper encircled its form.

From its place in the darkness, the rabbit could feel the sway of the man's body. It could smell the odor of stale sweat lining the inside of the cloth pocket, carrying a pungent memory of the compost pile outside of the potter's shed.

The potter's scent was different. His was the smell of salt-tinged sweat; little rivulets of it slipped down his arms and face as he turned, like rainwater on a craggy stone. The potter's scent was damp leaves, the hidden skin of pine bark, the soil beneath the cucumber vines, newly sprung mushrooms, dried moss in the deep wood. The potter was connected to the earth.

The clay was moving away from its home now. It could feel the distance yawning wider and wider. The wheel where it was birthed was gone. The movement was too fast, things passed by in a blur of senses. It could feel the air changing, filling with too many scents of man. Polluted, tainted.

The rabbit was afraid. There were too many noises. Voices were raised. A woman was shouting, shrilly, like a jay yelling over the ledge of its nest. Lights seeped in through the newspaper but the rabbit felt more than saw the slow movement of shadows. Then it was placed inside another cloth and felt the binding of tape wind around its body. The hands were gone. All was still.

The rabbit could not detect any sound, any sight, any smell. It had been made prisoner within a cave of darkness. There was no hum of the potter's wheel or music from his radio. There was no firefly glow from his swinging bulb or the afternoon sunlight leaning in through the shed window like a heavy branch. The other forms of clay, the brothers and sisters, were not here to provide warmth and memory in the night.

The clay was lost.

It longed to be back in the riverbed where the darkness was innocent. If it could return to the moist womb of its mother, it could be comforted by the weight of water and see the broken stars swimming above. It longed for escape, to be unknowing, unborn, unmade. But it had lost its power. The man who took it did not hear the calling.

In the darkness, the clay was forgotten.

Chapter 6

Throughout the civilized history of mankind, after the gradual change from nomadic hunter and gatherer to settled farmer and animal breeder, clay has probably been the most consistently used material for improving the quality of life.

—Robin Hopper, from *Functional Pottery Form and Aesthetic in Pots of Purpose*

On another humid Monday morning, Molly sat in the newspaper's break room, jotting notes on the Staunton collection. She liked the buzz of peripheral noise as other staffers talked and snacked around the gurgling coffee pot.

She needed as much help as possible to shut out the other buzzing in her head—the questions about George-Bradley's death and the whereabouts of his missing pottery.

Clayton, the self-titled Queen of Advertising, marched into the room and sat down across from her.

"Well, Miss Thang," Clayton began, rolling up the sleeves of his silk peach sweater, "I've heard some tantalizing news about you."

Aside from being the most flamboyant dresser and the bread and butter of the paper, Clayton was an infamous gossip. Molly had exchanged some catty comments with him about their boss, and though Clayton might sling a few verbal barbs around the break room, he was a kindhearted, loyal, and generous man.

Slicking his salt-and-pepper hair into place, Clayton leaned back and examined her. "I do declare, Miss Molly, you have a crush on Matt Harrison."

Molly squirmed in her chair and did her best to look preoccupied with her notepad.

"Don't even try that act with me. You know I have supersensitive radar when it comes to this kind of thing. Besides, a little birdie told me y'all went to dinner together."

"Clayton, it was just a working date."

"But you wish it was more, don't you? He is a fine-looking specimen of a man!"

"Shhh!" Molly pleaded in a whisper as another staff member came in. "So you found me out. What are you going to do with this information?"

"Darling! What do you think of me? And why look so glum? If I had your eyes and your complexion, I'd drive straight to Hollywood and demand my own decorating show. I'd get it too."

"Thanks, Clayton, but I've got some extra curves you don't have."

"Honey, you've got more curves than a mountain road and there's not a thing wrong with them. Marilyn Monroe was no stick figure. There's no such thing as an anorexic icon! Don't look now but I have seen your man checking out your—" He bit off the end of his sentence as Matt entered the room carrying a brown bag in one hand and chopsticks in the other.

"Hi, you two. Care for some Chinese?" he asked.

"A man who eats fatty foods. You are so sexy, Matt Harrison." Clayton twirled Matt's tie around his finger. "Is this a Burberry? Oh, you just get more and more delicious!"

Matt nodded in assent and smiled. "Thanks. Plates for you both?"

"Oh, no, not for me!" Clayton trilled. "I've had so many frozen mochas I just can't sit still." He sauntered off, whistling.

"Molly?"

"Sure." She grinned, pleased to be alone with him once again.

As he helped himself to pieces of sesame chicken and steaming white rice, Matt asked Molly what she was working on. She told him all about the visit to the Staunton mansion. She tried to explain how fine the antiques were, but Matt was more interested in the architecture of the house and in Bunny's phone call.

"Do you know who was on the other end of the line?" he asked.

"I'm not sure. Not a friend. Maybe an insurance agent or lawyer," Molly said. "She was adamantly defending the fact that she hadn't given her husband more than his usual dose of insulin."

"Maybe she was talking to a doctor."

"Because of the additional insulin found in his body?" she asked.

"Yes. There must have been enough to catch someone's attention," Matt suggested.

"I still say he'd never overdose on purpose."

Matt frowned. "But didn't you say his marriage was on the rocks? If Bunny didn't inject George-Bradley, maybe it was self-administered."

"Their marriage has been strained for years. Why would he commit suicide because of that *now*? He could have just gotten divorced. He wouldn't need to kill himself. Plus, I think the person who really suffered in that marriage was Bunny."

"Why do you say that?"

Molly told him about the photographs. "It was like she was creating a dream world. She had all these smiling pictures of her and George-Bradley, like they were the perfect couple. Poor thing. Her biggest fault was that she didn't like his stuff. She probably never thought her indifference to his collection would eventually doom their relationship."

"I do feel sorry for her. Still, she seems to have woken up from her dream world if she's selling all of his belongings this quickly. Seems to have recovered pretty fast, if you ask me."

Molly swallowed a delicious bite of spring roll. "Just in his part of the house. I bet that when she redecorates, she puts up more pictures and creates a kind of mausoleum to their marriage."

"People will do anything to get over losing someone . . ." Matt murmured, turning his face away.

Molly saw that he had suddenly withdrawn but couldn't figure out what she had said to drive him away. She tried to draw him back by wondering aloud, "But that still leaves the questions of the overdose and his missing pottery."

"The pottery could be anywhere, and who knows what was going on in his mind the morning he took those shots," Matt said flatly.

"You should have seen how he kept the pottery. It was perfectly arranged, labeled, and routinely dusted. It's missing. I feel it. Do you think George-Bradley's mistress, Susan, snuck into their house? There's something fishy about the double insulin injection theory, too. I saw something in George-Bradley's face, Matt. He was surprised in the end. Shocked. You can't easily shock a man like that," she stated animatedly. "There's been foul play, I know it in my gut, and I'm going to try to find out what happened."

"How?" he asked, looking at her curiously.

"I don't know, but I'm supposed to be doing these articles, so I have an excuse to interview people in his circle. I'm going to call some of the suspects from the kiln opening, like Susan Black. It seems that many people hated George-Bradley and it just so happens Swanson has me meeting with my first source of inside information tomorrow, twelve o'clock sharp. That's when I will be interviewing a rival collector, a man named Hillary Keane. George-Bradley cut him in line *and* insulted him. He ought to have a great deal to say," Molly stated resolutely.

Matt smiled at her stubbornness and laid a tentative hand on her arm. "Just be careful. Curiosity can get you into trouble, especially if you happen to be right and this man's death was no accident."

Puzzled by Matt's abrupt swing in mood, Molly was nonetheless delighted by his tender smile and the feel of his hand on her arm. She felt like it was burning heat right into her.

• • •

Molly loved her days off. On Sundays she'd often hang out with Clara or Kitty. Tuesday was the day to spend all morning in pajamas with coffee and a good book. Her two cats, Merlin and Griffin, would curl up on the sofa with her as she lounged about, reading and watching the Weather Channel.

This Tuesday could not follow the usual pattern. She had her interview with Hillary Keane at noon and needed to fight off her lethargy with a shower and strong coffee.

Her cats eyed her with disappointment as she came downstairs dressed for the day.

"Sorry, guys." She gave them each a pile of treats. "Mom's got to work today."

Because Molly's mind was filled with possible interview questions, the ride to Asheboro felt shorter than usual. Molly consulted the directions Swanson had written in his illegible scrawl and turned off a back road just south of Greensboro. Winding through the countryside, she felt her spirits lift. She was excited about comparing Hillary Keane's collection with George-Bradley's. And she couldn't stop thinking about the spark she'd felt when Matt had touched her arm. She turned up the oldies station and sang along with Elvis to "Viva Las Vegas."

A few miles north of Asheboro, she turned onto a smaller street lined with single-story brick homes and two-story bungalows from the 1960s. The lots were large and covered by massive trees and rolling lawns, but the houses were rather dingy and not as well kept as Molly had expected. Disappointed, she searched for house numbers, knowing that a ranch-style house could only hold so much pottery.

The last residence on the street belonged to Hillary Keane and Molly's hopes were restored. A large white colonial, the house looked down on the street from its green crest and yawned widely with a columned mouth. Surrounded by trimmed rhododendron and azalea bushes, the house looked quite comfortable perched above the other homes in the neighborhood. As Molly pulled up the driveway, she admired the large bed of rose bushes to the left and a neat brick walkway lined with an explosion of impatiens leading up to the front door.

The driveway led her to the back of the house, where a wide, low porch extended out onto the lawn. Molly parked in front of the garage, surprised that it was big enough to hold three cars. She wondered what Keane did for a living in order to afford multiple cars in addition to a large pottery collection.

Walking around to the front door, she noticed that the grass was not as neat as the garden beds. Despite the lack of rain, it had grown tall and was long overdue for a trim. Molly rang the doorbell and waited, going over her mental checklist of necessary supplies: mini-recorder, pad of paper with questions, pen, and camera. When no one came to the door and Molly didn't hear the sounds of footsteps from within the house, she rang again. She could hear the loud chimes echo inside, but no one responded to the bell.

She decided to try the back door. No answer. She checked her watch. It was exactly noon. Maybe Swanson had set the appointment for a different day. He had made scheduling errors before.

Stepping up onto the porch, Molly noticed a pair of parched ferns and a strewn pile of local newspapers around the welcome mat. She picked one up. It was the *Washington Post*. Hillary had left five days' worth of papers scattered about. Molly frowned. She hated things to be untidy.

Opening the screen door, she knocked on the wood interior door, growing irritated over having given up her day off for no reason. As she stepped back from the door in surrender, a scrap of paper fluttered out from its place between the two doors. She picked it up and read:

Sunday

Hey, Buddy,
Where are you? We had a tee time for this morning.
Did you forget? Stopped by here to pick you up, but no one was home. I called you on your cell, at home, and at work, but no dice. I don't know what's going on, but let's reschedule for next weekend. Give me a call.
—Gil

Molly stuck the note underneath the grip of the door knocker and then peered in one of the porch windows. She could see into the kitchen, where three of the Meaders roosters stood guard from their prominent place on top of the cabinets, but nothing struck her as odd. A mug sat out on the counter next to some brown bananas. Turning back to the drive, she looked again at the papers and the unkempt lawn.

Molly walked over to the garage and tried the door. It was locked. Peering in through the square windows of the garage doors, she could see that only one of the garage bays was occupied. A small, inexpensive pickup truck sat next to an empty bay, while the third was taken up by a large worktable surrounded by tools. Molly assumed Hillary Keane kept his other car in the second bay, so nothing looked out of place in the garage. Except for the rows of cardboard boxes carefully arranged on shelves lining the entire back wall. Whatever was in those boxes took up a great deal of space.

Molly moved over to the far bay, hoping to get a better view of the back wall from a different angle. From this vantage point, she could see that several of the shelves were empty, but there were rectangular-shaped clean spaces in the dust, indicating that boxes had once been stored there. The box closest to her had obviously been looked at recently, because the newspaper had not been completely replaced. No longer obscured by the classified section, the necks of two large pottery jugs jutted out from their nest. The rows and rows of packed boxes all contained pottery!

But why would Hillary Keane keep all his pottery out here, out of sight? Pottery collectors loved to touch and see their objects of desire. How had Keane planned to *show* her his collection if it was all buried out here in the garage?

She walked back toward her car and dialed the office. Swanson's secretary informed her that he was home with a cold and gave her his home number. She knew that there was a good chance her "sick" boss would be out fishing, but he answered his phone with an angry grunt.

"Carl? It's Molly."

"This better be good," he grumbled. "I've got a nasty cold, you know."

"Sorry to hear that. I'm at Hillary Keane's house, for our appointment, but he's not here."

"And what would you like me to do about that?" Swanson demanded.

"I'm just checking to make sure this is the correct day," Molly said carefully.

"Of course it is!" he barked. "I talked to him on Thursday, the day before the Burle kiln opening. He said he was thrilled to be able to show off his collection. Really wanted to help spread the word about the local potters. Seemed like a decent guy."

"Well, maybe he had to leave town. What should I do now?"

Swanson sighed. "I'll call my friend and see if he knows what happened to Keane."

"His name wouldn't be Gil, would it?" Molly asked.

"No, it's Bryant. Why?"

"Keane was supposed to play golf with Gil on Sunday. There's a note here from him. Apparently, Keane missed his tee time."

Uninterested, Swanson replied, "Ah, that's where I'm going right now. I need *something* to get my mind off of this cold."

Molly hung up and returned to her sweltering car. As she reversed down the driveway, the house seemed to be watching her through the streaked sunlight. It seemed especially silent on its lonely hill. Molly suddenly remembered how George-Bradley had cut in front of Keane at C.C.'s kiln opening. The look of outrage in Keane's eyes was unforgettable. Had George-Bradley stepped on Keane's toes more than once? Molly had a strong feeling that something was wrong in Hillary Keane's life, and it was more serious than a head cold.

One thing she felt with conviction. Whatever had caused Hillary Keane's absence was linked to those boxes of pottery.

• • •

On the ride home, Molly called her mother to see if she wanted to go out for dinner. Clara told her she was settled in a lounge chair reading, and that only her interest in hearing about Hillary Keane's collection could tear her away from the mystery she was reading.

"How's Lord Menes doing?" Molly asked after the novel's hunky Egyptian hero. She had already plowed through the series of five books.

"Handsome as ever. Every other paragraph is about his tan, muscular torso. I can't stand it."

"What will you do once you're finished?"

Her mother sighed longingly. "I'll just have to reread all the Horatio Hornblower books to keep me satisfied. How was your interview?"

"Didn't happen."

"What do you mean?"

Molly told her mother about her visit to Hillary Keane's.

"The pottery was packed in cardboard boxes?" Clara asked, completely perplexed. "What's the point of having such beautiful and interesting pieces of art hidden from view?"

"Maybe Keane just liked to hoard stuff. My boss said he sounded like a nice enough guy when they talked on the phone," Molly said.

"It's the South. Everyone sounds kind and cordial on the phone. Doesn't mean they can't snap at you like a rabid dog if duly provoked."

"True, but I may never find out. Carl is trying to locate Keane and will call me back tonight."

"What are we doing for dinner?" Molly heard the sound of fabric stretching and imagined Clara leaning all the way back on her lounge chair, her long legs crossed as she set her novel aside. "It's too hot to cook. Let's go to Panchos."

Molly laughed. "Excellent idea. I could use a margarita. After all, this *was* my day off."

• • •

Panchos was one of the few restaurants in Hillsborough. It had had a slow start, opening its doors in a town where people had been eating grits and barbeque all their lives. But it hadn't taken long for the delicious and inexpensive Mexican food to seduce the taste buds of even the least risk-taking eaters around.

Molly and Clara ordered jumbo margaritas on the rocks and dug into the warm tortilla chips and spicy salsa.

"Time to talk about serious matters," Molly began, swallowing a sip of her chilled delight. "There is something rotten in the state of North Carolina."

"Such as?"

Molly pushed the basket of chips toward her mother. "George-Bradley's death, for starters. Bunny was adamant that she gave him his daily insulin shot. On top of that, there's the missing pottery."

"Lex is going back over to the Staunton place tomorrow. He'll ask the cleaning lady if she knows anything and one mystery will be solved. As for the insulin issue, what are you suggesting?"

"What if someone gave George-Bradley more insulin? Someone who knew he had diabetes and knew his habits well enough to know that he'd already had one shot."

"You're still fixated on the possibility of *murder*?" Clara asked loudly.

At that awkward moment, the waitress arrived to take their orders. Clara chose a vegetarian plate with two bean burritos and a cheese enchilada. Molly skipped the beans and opted for three cheese enchiladas.

"I need my calcium," she told the waitress sheepishly. Turning back to her mother, she answered, "Yes, I do believe George-Bradley was murdered."

"Who are your suspects?"

As a plate of sizzling fajitas passed them by, Molly suggested that either Bunny or Susan could be the killer.

"I don't know," Clara pondered. "Susan wasn't exactly chasing after him at the kiln opening. I don't even think she'd want him back as a boyfriend. What reason would she have to kill him? I think Bunny had more motive."

Molly rubbed salt from the rim of her glass. "But what about all of those pictures Bunny had of them together? They were so nostalgic. And a little sad. She could have still loved her husband."

"Those photos don't mean *anything*," Clara said dismissively. "They were probably put out just for show. Bunny wouldn't let it *seem* like she and George-Bradley were anything but happy. I doubt her closest friends knew if there was anything wrong in that marriage. Bunny cares about appearances."

"She didn't bother concealing how she felt when we were there."

"That's because we don't count as people who matter. We're the *help*."

"So what about Hillary Keane's anger at the kiln opening? Keane knew George-Bradley, I could tell by the look he gave our victim. And what about Keane blowing off both my interview and his golf buddy? The man is gone, I tell you."

"He had to leave town. He'll turn up. Look, as much as I love a good mystery, I don't think there is one here."

As the waitress arrived with scalding plates of food, Molly's phone chirped from within her purse. She quickly grabbed it and made for the door. It was a pet peeve of hers that people had loud phone conversations in restaurants, and she vowed never to be so impolite.

"Hello?"

Her boss coughed in her ear. "Seems that Keane really has disappeared. He hasn't been to work for the last couple of days and my friend hasn't heard a word from him either. Says the two of them are pretty close, too. He's actually going to call the police. In the meantime, why don't you interview that potter who used to visit your school? You told me about him last year."

"Sam Chance? I would love to see him again." Molly was thrilled. Swanson was lining up another person who had been to the kiln opening. However, she thought of one drawback. "Just so you know, Sam produces mostly functional pottery. Nothing fancy."

"That's fine. We want to represent a varied mix of potters. It's not like people don't collect dishes . . ."

"True. I'm also hoping to arrange an interview with Susan Black, another collector. I left a message on her answering machine but haven't heard anything yet . . . Listen, is Keane married?" Molly asked.

"Nope, he's a bachelor, unlike me. And my wife is calling me for supper."

"Wait!" Molly caught him. "Just tell me one more thing. What is Keane's profession?"

"He's a pharmacist."

Molly snapped her cell phone closed and rejoined her mother.

"Let's examine one of the suspects on my list," she told Clara proudly.

"Okay. According to you, we have Bunny the jealous wife, Susan the vengeful mistress, and now . . . ?"

"Hillary Keane."

"What did your boss say?" Clara asked.

"Keane has officially gone missing. Hasn't been home, hasn't been to work, and no one seems to know where he is. The police are being called in to investigate."

"And why does that make him a suspect?"

"Because of his job. He's a pharmacist!" Molly exclaimed.

Clara sat back in her chair and sipped her drink thoughtfully. Then her eyes widened. "He's got access to insulin."

"Exactly. And maybe he gave himself access to some of George-Bradley's pottery. That could explain the *where* in our 'where has the pottery gone?' question."

"All right, for argument's sake let's assume Keane wanted to knock off George-Bradley and take some pieces, how would he give him the extra insulin? I saw him at the kiln opening, but only for a moment."

"I don't know. I'd have to ask Matt for some ideas."

Clara's glass stopped in midair on the way to her mouth. "Matt?"

"Oh, he works with me at the paper." Molly tried to keep from blushing, but Clara sensed there was more to be discovered about this coworker.

"Why would your coworker know about diabetes?" she asked.

"He went to med school for three years. He knows quite a bit," Molly defended Matt, and then quickly changed the subject. "Back to Keane."

Clara put up her hand to stop her daughter from continuing. "If Keane *had* stolen pottery he could never put the pieces on display."

Molly jerked her fork in the air. "Thus the boxes in the garage!"

Clara was still doubtful. "He'd be taking a significant risk to hoard away a bunch of stolen pieces. Someone would know."

"Maybe he was selling them."

"That's possible." Clara thought for a moment. "He could be selling up north to buyers who wouldn't know the provenance of the pieces. They'd have no idea they were writing checks for stolen goods. But Keane couldn't use an online auction or anything on the Internet; people around here would recognize every jug and pitcher and know whose collection they belonged to."

The two women mused over their theories. Riddles circulated like pesky summer flies.

"The real question is"—Molly paused for emphasis—"who would know more about the relationship between George-Bradley and Hillary Keane? If one of them bore a grudge against the other, maybe we can link this all up."

"I'll call Donald." Clara signaled the waitress for the check. "He knows everyone in the pottery circle. If there's a person alive who knows the intimate details of the connection between George-Bradley and Keane, it's Donald."

Without a doubt, Clara's friend Donald had the largest and most valuable Southern pottery collection of the region. His collection was even larger and more impressive than George-Bradley's. Unlike his former rival, Donald also supported the potters in other ways in addition to buying their wares. He helped them market their pieces and even lent them money to open their own shops after completing an apprenticeship.

Donald attended almost every area kiln opening, bought at auction, and made deals with other collectors. His trade was in the jewelry business, but his real love was pottery. He and Clara had met over ten years ago at a sale and had become fast friends. Now they helped each other track down unusual pieces for their collections and often invested in pieces together that were later sold at the region's largest pottery show for a tidy profit. When Donald wasn't selling jewelry, he was out "beating the bushes" for pottery. He knew everyone who owned so much as a clay ashtray.

"Will you call him tonight?" Molly asked hopefully.

Clara looked at her watch. "No, it's too late. Donald's an early-to-bed, early-to-rise type of gentleman. It will have to wait until tomorrow. By then, Lex will have found out if the pottery is somewhere else in the Stauntons' house and maybe we can tie up some loose ends."

"I'll have to settle for tomorrow then." Molly sighed, getting up. "Just think, Ma. If we could solve this mystery I could write the best article *Collector's Weekly* has ever seen. It would make my earlier pieces about ghost bidding and online fraud look like small change!" On the way to the car she put her arm around her mother's waist and squeezed. "My coworkers would look at me in a whole new light."

Molly was especially interested in impressing a particular coworker. It was about time she did something to make Matt Harrison notice her.

Chapter 7

Brother, stay here;
Are we not brothers?
So man and man should be,
But clay and clay differs in dignity,
Whose dust is both alike.

—William Shakespeare, *Cymbeline*

Molly was scrubbing the bathtub when the phone rang. She turned off the water, wiped her hands hastily on the bath mat, and grabbed the receiver, water dripping down her arm and onto the carpet.

"Hello?" she asked abruptly.

"My, my, aren't we crabby? And what are you doing home on a Wednesday?"

"Sorry, Ma. I was just bleaching the bathtub. Griffin peed in it again last night. That cat is so lazy. It's not like he doesn't have a cat door! Can you hold on for a sec?" Molly peeled off her yellow rubber gloves and wiped her arms with a cloud-white bath towel. "I'm using the time I wasted yesterday to clean house and run errands. What's up?"

"Lots, and it cost me lunch."

"You saw Donald today?" Molly asked.

"Yes. I took him to his favorite Chinese place and mercilessly pumped him for information." Clara laughed mischievously.

"And?"

"Well, he didn't want to tell me anything at first. Hillary, George-Bradley, and Donald—all these guys grew up together so they're often reluctant to tell stories about one another."

"Even to you? You and Donald gossip about everyone. You're like two senior citizens at the hair salon."

"I know, that's why it was strange that he was so reticent, but don't worry, I finally wormed some juicy tidbits from him." Clara paused, obviously baiting her daughter.

"Go on!" Molly prompted excitedly.

"Well, back in the early days of George-Bradley's collecting, he and Keane used to go to kiln openings and auctions together. They knew each other during their junior high days, drifted apart during college, and were kind of reacquainted through pottery. Problem was, they both liked the same pieces. George-Bradley could afford them. Keane could purchase a good piece every now and then, but more often than not, he had to watch as George-Bradley bought up all the best pieces."

"So he began getting jealous."

"Yes. But according to Donald, it took a few years to bubble to the surface. From the outside, you'd never know that those two weren't the perfect buddies. They went to each other's parties, traveled to shows out of state together, and were generally thought to be best friends."

"What happened?"

Clara sighed. "This is the part where Donald got fidgety. Apparently, Keane started dropping by George-Bradley's house—often when his friend wasn't at home. Keane would tell Bunny that he'd wait in the living room for her husband to return. Sometimes he was still there when George-Bradley got back from work or wherever, but other times, he wasn't."

"Because he was stealing pottery!" Molly exclaimed.

"That's what George-Bradley thought too. He noticed a piece missing after one of Keane's visits. Donald was at a swank party given for members of the Southern Pottery Collectors Group when he overheard the two friends go at it. George-Bradley accused Keane of taking some of his pieces while he was out of the house—pieces that Keane had always coveted."

"Did Keane make a scene?"

"Not really. Donald said Keane got really red in the face and told George-Bradley in an outraged whisper that their years of friendship obviously meant nothing if he was being called a thief by the one man he thought of as a *brother*."

"How dramatic."

"Exactly. George-Bradley didn't bother apologizing. They just stared daggers at each other. Then Keane downed his drink and left the party."

"But they still must have run into each other all the time after that. The world of pottery collectors is fairly small and intimate."

"Donald says you couldn't tell they even knew each other from the way they acted after that party. He only knows the truth because he was standing close enough to overhear their argument."

"How long ago did they stop being friends?" Molly asked.

"A couple years now."

Molly tried to picture the scene at the party. "So after he stopped bumming around with Keane, did George-Bradley start finding women to accompany him to sales and shows instead?"

"I guess."

"There you have it. Keane's a prime suspect!" Molly declared. "However, there's a detail that I need to discover in order to confirm my suspicions."

Clara cleared her throat. "What's that?"

"Well, I've been thinking. Matt told me that George-Bradley suffered from an insulin overdose at the kiln opening. But I wonder, with all that sugary food, *plus* sweet tea, wouldn't he have had enough sugar to balance out the insulin even if he gave himself an extra dose? If he *had* taken two shots, he must have had the second one well before he arrived and ate all that sugar."

Clara considered this. "So you need to find out where George-Bradley was before the kiln opening?"

"If he was only with Bunny then she's my number-one suspect," Molly continued. "Though it's pretty suspicious that Keane flew the coop right after George-Bradley's death. Perhaps Keane and Bunny were in it together," Molly added, though she didn't really subscribe to this theory. "She hated the pottery. Keane coveted it."

Clara ignored the latter bits of her daughter's speculations. "You'll have to ask Bunny if George-Bradley was home right up until the time he left for the kiln opening. I don't know how you'd bring that up in conversation with her."

"Me either," Molly confessed. She thanked her mother and then dialed Matt's extension at the office.

"I am so glad you're in," she gushed when he answered.

"Wow, thanks," Matt replied happily.

"I've got a medical question for you."

"And here I thought just the sound of my voice made you weak in the knees," he teased.

Molly took a deep breath and threw caution to the wind. "It does," she recklessly admitted. And then, she hastily continued before he could reply. "Listen, if George-Bradley had taken two shots of insulin, wouldn't a handful of cookies and a big glass of sweet tea negate the overdose?"

"Depends on how much extra insulin we're taking about. It could certainly slow down any negative side effects—enough to get him to the hospital for treatment."

"So that's a 'yes'?"

"It depends on how many units he took with each shot. If that second shot were a much higher dose, there'd be a bigger risk of death."

"And who would know how many units he regularly took besides his doctor?" Molly asked.

Matt paused to think. "His pharmacist, I suppose."

"His pharmacist," Molly repeated.

"Are you still playing detective?" he asked breezily, and she related all of her suspicions to him while trying not to sound like a fool.

"The biggest hole in my theory revolves around the question of how Keane could give George-Bradley the extra insulin." Molly was grateful that Matt was taking her seriously. "And why kill his former friend now? Did Keane want to steal more pottery? Was he having financial problems?"

"George-Bradley took a shot to get his insulin. I'd think he'd notice if someone stuck him with a needle," Matt pointed out.

Realization hit Molly on the head like a flying brick. "But that's it!" she shouted excitedly. "That's why he was rubbing his stomach. He wasn't doing that because he had just given himself a shot. Bunny always did that for him at home. No. Someone stuck him at the kiln opening! There was such a rush of people bumping into one another . . . it was the perfect opportunity. Keane was there, and he has access to insulin."

"Molly, it would have to be a *huge* dose to cause the reaction it did. Do you have any other evidence?"

"Not yet. I'm going to interview my friend Sam Chance tomorrow. I'll see if he can tell me anything we don't already know about George-Bradley or Hillary Keane. Plus, he was at the kiln opening and he always has his ear to the ground."

"Is he a potter or collector?"

Molly smiled over the phone. "A potter and one of the nicest people I've ever met."

"Have a good trip," Matt said warmly. "And let me know if . . . um . . . if you get stuck . . . I could be your Watson."

"Well, Doctor," Molly replied coyly, her heart singing, "you may just get the job."

Chapter 8

And life is much faster now than ours was. It's harder for young people to get into this business because they don't have the time to apprentice long enough to learn it. They've got to start earning a living right away and have a big paycheck to apply to the expenses of rising prices.

—Louis Brown, Arden, North Carolina, pottter, from *Foxfire 8*

Chance's Ware was in Seagrove, off the beaten path. Molly had plenty of time to spare, so she took a detour before her interview. Donald had told Clara over a bowl of steamed dumplings that Keane worked at the pharmacy downtown. That could only mean downtown Asheboro. Molly looked in the phone book and discovered only two pharmacies within city limits. She figured she could find the right one.

Her strategy was simple: find out exactly when Keane took off and if anyone had noticed him acting strangely before he left the area. She planned to pretend to be a friend delivering a piece of pottery who hadn't heard a thing about Keane's disappearance. Molly had a weak poker face, so she prayed she could carry this off or her detective work would meet a quick end.

The pharmacy closest to the highway was a small brick building on the corner. Urns of pink petunias turned their faces up to greet the rays of sun bouncing off the store windows in a wash of white light. The parking lot was swept clean and a little bell trilled out her arrival as she opened the paneled door.

She spotted a red and white sign that read Prescriptions in the back of the store. A girl who looked as though she should still be in high school filed orders into alphabetical bins. She crackled bubble gum in time to the store's jazzy elevator music, blowing large, pink balloons and then sucking them back into her mouth with a series of snaps and pops. Her dirty blonde hair, held back in a ponytail, swung back and forth like a pendulum as she moved from bin to bin.

Molly took a breath and approached her. "Excuse me."

The girl swung around, her hair whipping over her shoulder. Her name tag read Brandy.

"Yeah?" She looked at Molly blankly.

"I'm looking for Mr. Keane," she said in her most sugary voice.

Brandy's eyes immediately narrowed and her jaw froze mid-chew. "He's not here," she said, and then added reluctantly, "Can I help you with somethin'?"

"No," Molly assured her. "I've come to deliver a piece of pottery to him."

"Sorry, he's not in," the girl replied flatly.

"But we were supposed to meet today," Molly insisted gently. "I drove all the way from Durham as a favor to him."

Brandy digested this bit of information while indecision played across her freckled face.

"Look." Her voice became strained. "He hasn't been to work for over a week. I don't know what else to tell you."

Molly dropped her eyes to the counter and frowned, doing her best to act worried. "Is he all right?"

The conspiring whisper and the concerned face drew Brandy in. "We don't know," the girl admitted, leaning closer. "He's *missing*."

"What?" Molly asked breathlessly, looking around the room wildly and hoping she wasn't overacting. "Since when?"

"Friday afternoon, I guess." The girl closed up again. She obviously cared for her boss on some level and wasn't willing to expose her feelings to a stranger.

Last Friday had been the day of the kiln opening. Molly swallowed her excitement. She reached across the counter, patted the girl's forearm, and replied tenderly, "You poor thing. You must be worried sick."

Brandy's anxiety washed over her face, making her appear even younger and more vulnerable. "I am," she confessed. "I worked with him that afternoon. He took the morning off to go to some pottery thing. But I was the last one to see him."

"You must have to get in here awfully early," Molly sympathized.

"Yeah, 'bout seven to get all the orders ready by openin' time," she sighed. "The cashiers don't have to be here 'til eight thirty, but we, I mean, Mr. Keane and me, we gotta be here early every single day."

"Do you always have the same shift?" Molly asked, an idea forming.

Brandy blew an enormous bubble and sucked it back into her mouth as she studied Molly. "Yeah. There's a pharmacist's assistant who works evenings, but he's always here by himself."

"Then you and Mr. Keane must be close, working side by side every day . . ." Molly suggested. She was hoping that showing a willingness to listen would get Brandy to confess something more intimate about her working relationship. Her intuition paid off.

The girl hesitated and her shoulders slumped. Finally, she said very softy, "We are. He hired me after I got . . . after I had some trouble. Not many people would do that. I really need this job."

"He is a good man," Molly agreed with false enthusiasm. She suddenly felt guilty about pumping this girl for information. Brandy might look young and innocent, but she had clearly had to grow up swiftly. Now her benefactor had disappeared, and the town was probably rife with rumor.

"I wouldn't worry," Molly said brightly, trying to ease the girl's mind. "Maybe he took a last-minute trip to get away from it all . . . did he seem stressed to you?"

The girl shook her head, her mind elsewhere.

"Well, these pottery people are always running off to some show or another." She felt another pang of guilt. "Did he act like he was excited about an upcoming event or . . . maybe worried about something?"

Brandy looked at her like she was the village idiot. "He's always worried! He has a good reason to be!"

What did that mean? Suddenly, an image flashed before Molly's eyes. She remembered Keane at the kiln opening, struggling to clean his glasses. Those hands. They had been so gnarled and his face had been filled with embarrassment and frustration. Molly had seen hands like that before. Her grandmother's sister, an accomplished pianist, had developed such bad arthritis in her early sixties that she could no longer play. Molly recalled a faint memory of the swollen knuckles, the disobedient fingers, and the agonized flush on her great aunt's face as she attempted to peel an apple over the sink.

"Of course," Molly whispered, more to herself than to the girl. "What pain he must have been in all the time."

Brandy responded to the genuine sympathy in Molly's voice. "He was. Even though he takes medicine, he can hardly open the pill bottles anymore." She looked around to make sure no one could overhear a confession that could ruin her mentor's career. "I have to use all the keys for him. It's too hard for him to fit them into the lock. The whole thing isn't fair, either. It's not like he's an old man, but he has such a serious case and he's afraid he'll have to retire if anyone reports him to the district manager."

Molly realized that Brandy was a little bit in love with her employer. "It's good of you to give Mr. Keane a hand," she said kindly. "He helped you, so now you keep his arthritis a secret. You make it so that he can still do his job. That's admirable, Brandy."

But Molly had gone too far in voicing Keane's affliction. Brandy gave her a guarded stare, mumbled, "Yeah," and returned back to her work and defensive gum chewing.

"Look, if I hear anything about his whereabouts, I'll call you," Molly offered, even though Brandy had turned away. "No matter what, you'll be just fine. You obviously have a good head on your shoulders."

Brandy raised her face and gave a slight nod. Molly retreated to her car, feeling like a complete jerk. Her theory about Keane had been shot to bits. If he had such an advanced case of arthritis that he couldn't open a bottle cap or turn a set of keys, there was no way he could squeeze the tiny syringe used to give George-Bradley the extra shot of insulin. But if Keane was innocent of the murder, why had he run away?

• • •

Molly stopped to pick up a dozen donuts. Sam Chance loved anything with sugar, and his apprentices were always hungry. Consulting her Seagrove area potteries map, she remembered that the landmark closest to Chance's Ware was the abandoned Chance Beans factory. The dilapidated building and overgrown lot proudly displayed a real estate sign. Molly was surprised to see that the sign read Sold.

Chance's Ware was down a long gravel road, much like a hundred other potters in the area. The yard was deserted except for the polished Ford pickup resting under a carport.

"Someone has a new truck." She greeted Sam with a hug as he came out of the workshop.

His kind face broke out into a wide grin, scattering laugh lines across his cheeks and carving creases into the corners of his blue eyes. "Yes, indeed." He rocked back on his heels, hands tucked into his overall pockets as the two of them admired the sheen of the vehicle.

"Did some Chance Beans relative leave you a pile after they sold their land?"

"Now you know I'm no kin to them. If I were, I'd be messin' around with clay for fun and wouldn't trouble over sellin' a pot. Nope," he said as he patted the hood of his truck affectionately, "bought this by sweat and tears."

"I brought you something to cure your sweet tooth," Molly said as she handed him the box of donuts.

"Oh, boy." Sam whistled. "This'll help, but my case is hopeless. Come on up to the shop."

They walked up the driveway to the metal-sided barn, which housed Sam's wheel, drying shelves, glaze barrels, and all the ware available for purchase. Molly looked around at his utilitarian pieces. He made plates, bowls, pitchers, candleholders, bean pots, casseroles, and birdhouses in four different glazes. His traditional pieces were concentrated on a single table, where several face jugs with corncob stoppers and a few roosters proudly proclaimed their creator's right as a fifth-generation potter.

"So what do you want to cover today? Lord knows I could talk pottery to you until the cows come home, but I don't figure you've got all that much time."

Molly watched as Sam helped himself to a jelly donut.

"How about digging the clay and turning? Unless you want to talk about firing too."

"Well, you've been to C.C.'s," Sam said, "so you've seen the best kiln around these parts. He's got the genuine article in that groundhog kiln of his."

"Let's cover how a piece of wet clay becomes a jug," Molly suggested.

"All the action before glazing."

"Right."

Sam dusted sugar particles from his overalls, pointing to a shelf of unglazed pots. "It's called bisque ware when the pottery hasn't been glazed yet. Lots of us say 'biscuit' for short."

"If it sounds like food, then I can remember it." Molly took a chocolate-frosted donut for herself. "Where are all your apprentices today?"

"Oh, they're delivering a load to some gardening place in Asheville. Lady bought up all my flowerpots and birdhouses except this one."

"That's great, Sam! And where's your talented son Justin, the famous sixth-generation Chance potter?"

A look of sadness surfaced in Sam's eyes, then darted away like a startled minnow. "He's going to law school."

"Oh. What does that mean for the future of your business?"

"Well, he's using the kiln at the university's main campus, so he hasn't quit pottery. But I don't think he's going to be a full-time potter. I can only hope that I live long enough to wait for him to retire from the law and take over the business."

Molly reassured her friend with a pat on the hand. "Maybe he just needs to spread his wings for a few years. He'll end up here eventually. And there aren't too many parents who'd complain about their kids becoming attorneys."

Sam smiled, his good humor restored. "I know it, but we're a dying breed out here. Some things are more important than money."

Sam led her down to the banks of the creek that snaked through long grasses and stooped trees. There, a large depressed circle formed a wide bog. Molly poked at the clay with a stick and asked Sam if he had stayed at C.C.'s long enough to see the collapse of George-Bradley.

"I sure did. The whole town is a-twitter over it. It's a shame, him being so young and all."

Calling George-Bradley young was a stretch, but Sam always had a kind word for everyone. Molly knew that George-Bradley wouldn't have bought much from Sam because he wasn't as collectible as many of the other potters, but it didn't affect the potter's disposition. But then, Molly suddenly remembered how rude George-Bradley had been to Sam at the kiln opening, slighting him for creating "pretty dinner plates" instead of traditional art pottery. Was it possible that Sam wanted revenge for having his life's work insulted so publicly?

"Weren't you angry at him for what he said to you that morning? He insulted your work." Molly watched Sam's face carefully as he replied, even though she didn't really believe Sam had the capacity to hurt anyone.

"Shoot." Sam shook his head. "I can't get in a huff just 'cause some big shot doesn't like what I make. Those dinner plates have sent my two boys to college, and we've had full bellies every day of our lives." He grinned nonchalantly, rubbing his small paunch.

"Now, back to business. This is our clay pit." He pointed at the bog. "We dig it, mix it up with some commercial clay, and add some water. That gives it a good, plastic feel. You gotta have that to turn."

"I bet you get some serious mosquitoes from that pit." Molly felt itchy just looking at it.

"I wear overalls for more than one reason," Sam laughed, leading her back toward the shop, where he pointed at a square machine the size of a refrigerator turned on its side.

"This is a motorized pug mill. It mixes the clay. Back in my daddy's day, they had a pug mill turned by a mule. Most people had those kind, but none of us keep mules anymore."

"Does this do a better job?"

"Not really, but we just got sick of puttin' that poor mule to work. Us kids were all crazy about that mule. She was our family pet." Sam rocked back on his heels, remembering.

"So she retired and lived a good life?"

"Not exactly. We stopped working her, and on her very first day of retired life she keeled over and died on us."

"That's a terrible story!" Molly laughed. "What did you call her?"

"Whiskey Girl. Whiskey jugs were real big when my daddy was turning. Everybody wanted one, especially with our corncobs stuck in 'em. So it seems like we heard that word about a million times a day."

Molly made a mental note to add the mule story to her article. "So what's next, after the clay gets mixed up?"

"Well, now you've gotta pick the junk out of it. You're gonna have all kinds of stuff in there. Stuff the screens don't get out. So you need to cut it up into slabs and pick it out."

Sam picked up a block of clay and sliced into it with a wire.

"Banjo string," he told her, cutting a bread-sized piece of clay that revealed embedded pieces of grass and stone.

"May I?" Molly helped herself to a slab and pulled out the invasive bits of nature. The clay was cool and moist, nestling comfortably in her hand.

"Now you've got to get it ready for the wheel. That means a good beating."

Molly jumped as Sam slapped their combined pieces onto the worktable. He picked up the mass, pushed it together, and slammed it down again and again.

"That looks positively therapeutic," Molly said.

"It helps after a weekend of not selling a single thing."

Once the clay was worked into the right plasticity, Sam slapped it on the wheel.

"This is the hard part." Sam gestured to her to approach the wheel. "Give it a try."

He issued instructions on how to use the foot pedal, and as she pushed down on it the wheel sprung into action, and the clay mass lunged sideways, seeking a means of escape.

"Whoa, slow down there," Sam laughed, easing her foot off the pedal. "Now let's give this guy a shower."

Molly cupped the clay lightly in her hands as Sam drizzled it with water. As she spun the wheel, it moved through her fingers like the smooth back of a snake.

"Now, you can't go gentle with it. Gotta treat it like a spoilt child due for a lickin'. Cup it hard with the insides of your palms, I'm gonna help you center it."

Sam guided her hands and touched places on her forearms where she needed to use some sleeping muscles to coax the clay to the center of the wheel. Molly was surprised at the strength it took to force the clay against its will to move from the spot where it was placed originally. Now she understood why all the potters had arms like Popeye the Sailorman.

"Good. Now I'm gonna open it up for you."

Sam leaned over the opposite side of the wheel with a tool comprised of a board with a metal ball in the middle. He pressured the ball into the top of the clay's mass, and an open mouth sprang into the clay's center, yawning crookedly as Molly tried to control the body with one hand and widen the mouth with the other. Her novice hands were no match for the clay. It bucked and kicked out like a rodeo pony, and she grew frustrated as she tried to bring it under the rein of her palms.

"This is *hard*," she said, forcing out a laugh. She was disappointed that she didn't have more skill.

"Yep. Takes years to really figure it all out. How does the clay feel?"

"Like it's alive. It sure has a mind of its own. I definitely respect it, but I'm mad at it too. It's not doing what's in my mind's eye."

Sam chuckled. "Well, that's your first lesson. You don't think when your hands are on the clay. You let go—your body moves its body."

Molly watched in a semi-hypnotic state as Sam pulled up her floppy bowl into an oblong shape and closed up the mouth into a thin neck. His hands moved slowly, with deliberate grace, and the clay immediately recognized him as a master and fell obedient.

"Let's put a handle on," he said.

Sam showed her how to slice a strip of clay for the handle. After he applied it to the jug, he slipped wire under the piece's bottom and picked it up with large, wooden tongs. The simple implements reminded Molly of how men had moved ice blocks one hundred years ago. It was an interesting image considering potters now used them to carry a wet, fragile vessel that could last for a century or more once it was burned by the kiln.

"Wanna make a face?" Sam asked.

"Sure, how about a devil?"

"We'll have to let the jug dry a bit first. Come on into the house and I'll show you my collection."

They gave their hands a cursory washing in the rain barrel and moved on up to the large log cabin nuzzling a grove of pines. Sam's collection was held in the front room. He showed her face jugs from his father's and grandfather's time and other family pieces dating before the Civil War. The greenish glaze, flaked with imperfections, was the same he now used. It looked much like C.C.'s, which made sense since both men worked together as apprentices when they were young.

On another bookcase, Sam had collected various pieces from other Seagrove potters. Molly recognized a Billy Ray Hussey lion and a water pitcher made by the Cole family, but the shelf of Jack Graham pieces immediately drew her attention away from all the others.

"I think he's wonderful," she said, admiring a crimson vase.

"These are early ones." Sam tilted the vase upside down to show her the kiln number. It was from kiln number five. That would be way back in the early eighties."

"You must have been at the same openings as George-Bradley. I just saw his collection."

Sam nodded. "Oh, sure, he'd never miss a Jack Graham sale."

"He missed number forty-three," Molly said.

Sam frowned, looking down on his collection. "I don't have any from that kiln opening either."

Molly started. Here were two men who never missed a Graham kiln opening, yet neither one had made it to the event debuting kiln forty-three?

"Was there something wrong with that batch?" she asked Sam.

A dark shadow passed across Sam's face, and without his customary smile, he suddenly looked older. He replaced the vase, hiding his exposed emotion by turning away from Molly.

"I just don't really recall. It was over two years ago." Sam's face was swept clean by the time he stood back up and gave her a little grin. Sam was lying—she could tell. What had he remembered at that moment about kiln forty-three?

Molly pointed to a humdrum brown vase that appeared to be identical to the two in George-Bradley's collection.

"Are those from later kilns?" she asked, amazed that the potter who had created such stunning work could suddenly produce something so bland.

"Yes. That's all he's made in the last two years. Brown vases. He gives them to C.C. to sell, but mostly a chain of florists from Winston-Salem buys them up. He doesn't sell to the public himself anymore. He's gone back to being a welder. Now," Sam said, obviously wanting to change the subject, "I've got some old Jugtown pieces on the bottom shelf, did you see those?"

Molly decided to press Sam just once more. "I would love to interview Jack. I want to see how he gets his forms so symmetrical," she said, trying to sound innocent.

Sam turned his gentle, frank face to her. "He's not gonna talk to you."

Molly was surprised by Sam's certainty. "Why not?"

"He just doesn't do interviews anymore."

"Oh." Molly wished the potter would offer more information, but he was moving toward the door. Not wanting to push her friend any further, Molly reminded Sam that her jug was incomplete.

Sam perked up and said, "Let's make that face."

Molly found she had some skill at creating the facial features. Using a knife, she cut ears, a nose, brows, and lips from a slice of clay. Sam showed her how to score, but he seemed distracted, his eyes wandering over to the edge of the woods. Memories were swarming around him like bees. She could practically hear them buzzing through the loops and curves of his cerebellum.

Molly applied two horns and poked shallow eyeholes using a pencil. Then Sam showed her how to cut pieces of broken dishes for the teeth. She made them especially jagged and pointy, to complement the devil's fierce scowl.

"When you're in town next, you can pick him up. What color do you want to glaze him?"

"Really?" Molly couldn't hide her pleasure. She decided to give the jug to Matt once it was fired. "A nice, deep blue. I'm going to give him to a coworker. He's a Duke Blue Devils fan."

"Oh, dear." Sam shook his head in mock sorrow. "There's only one basketball team in this state, and I believe they're called the UNC Tarheels."

Molly swept her arm around the building and said, "Well, I see some devils here, but I don't see a single ram."

"I'll get right to work on that." Sam laughed heartily.

Molly cleaned herself off again and got ready to go. She thanked Sam for his time and for introducing her to the wheel.

"You oughta give it a shot. Takes some time to get used to, but it's hard to stop once you start."

Molly shook her head. "I like it, I just don't think I'd be any good."

"It's in you, I can tell," Sam said seriously.

Molly glowed. "I think I will look into taking a class at the Cultural Arts Center. Thanks, Sam."

He walked her to her car, hands in overall pockets.

"Molly," Sam said as he opened her car door, "Jack Graham won't give interviews because he and his wife had some real trouble a couple of years ago. It's changed him. He's not the same man he used to be. I'm just telling you so you don't go callin' him."

Molly couldn't tell whether he was worried for her sake or for Jack's.

"All right, I won't," she promised.

He seemed relieved. Backing down the driveway, she waved at the small, sweet man in mud-stained overalls.

Back on the main road, Molly's brain was spinning. Something happened with kiln number forty-three, but what? Was it an event that would make a good article? Or was it something more sinister?

Sam's phrase followed after her like a cloud of dust: *They had some real trouble. It's changed him.*

Trouble.

The word rumbled through her air conditioner and overpowered the music from the radio. It sat in the stifling air under the black leather seats and fogged up the windows with its weighted humidity. Molly rolled down the windows to let it out, but it refused to budge.

Chapter 9

The way of clay is to understand the nature of clay, its wonderful plastic response when handled with love and care, and its collapse and disintegration when maltreated, overworked and strained beyond its capabilities.

—Harry Memmott, from *Discovering Pottery*

Inspired by her trip to Sam's, Molly headed for the closest megasized bookstore to learn more about the background of pottery making. Armed with a stack of heavy books and a cinnamon latte, Molly passed the afternoon lazily as she read up on wheel techniques, kiln building, and glaze recipes.

As Molly sat drinking her second cup of overpriced coffee, two young women sat down next to her and began poring hungrily over bridal magazines. One of them had apparently just gotten engaged and the other was her future maid of honor. Molly was distracted by their cries of "Look at this one!" as they ogled expensive dresses or squealed over the leg-of-mutton sleeves on some awful, fuchsia-hued bridesmaid dress.

Soon, the floor space between their two tables was littered with a pile of books and magazines opened to glossy pages of glowing brides, flower-rimmed wedding cakes, and glittering engagement rings the size of small icebergs. Molly glanced down at one of the magazine covers featuring an article called "Fashion for Older Brides: Ages 30–40."

She frowned. "Older" was age thirty? She would already be considered an older bride. Ridiculous. Molly sighed, thinking of her mother's persistent nagging fear of her daughter becoming a spinster. Molly didn't want to be a spinster either, but she certainly wasn't going to settle for Mr. So-So just to become a Mrs. So-So.

The former gloom of the day settled back on her shoulders like a cloak. First, there was Sam's warning to stay away from Jack Graham. Now, in a haven of books and caffeine that usually formed a comforting setting, Molly felt out of place. The pile of bridal magazines pointedly reminded her of her single status, and the magnificent sparkle of her neighbor's ring caught her eye with each excited wave of the girl's manicured hand. Every table in the cafe seemed to be occupied by chatting couples or smug women with wedding bands. Molly sighed. It was time to go.

Perhaps a connection with Matt was in order. If she could just get him out of the office again, they might have a chance to get to know each other better. Molly envisioned a candlelit table with Matt listening raptly to her witty conversation. Yes! She could take charge and ask *him* out. Molly had never asked a man on a date before and she was terrified, but why not give it a shot? After all, women now performed all kinds of feats once reserved for men. Gender roles were being redefined all the time.

Driving back to the newspaper's office building, she pictured Matt's laughing blue eyes and his easy smile. She thought about his calmness and the way he listened so attentively to everything she said. Fueled by determination, she checked her flawless complexion in the lobby mirrors, ran her fingers through her dark hair, and made her way to her desk with brisk, confident strides.

She decided to quickly check her voice mail before sailing off into the evening's sunset with Matt. She only had one message, and it was from Susan Black.

"Miss Appleby?" Susan's cool voice hummed through the receiver. "I received your message about doing an interview on my collection. Of course"—she made an effort to sound less frosty—"I would love to oblige, but I'd like to wait until after the Lex Lewis auction this weekend. You see, I plan to enhance my collection by adding several notable pieces from that sale. So let's plan on the week after, all right? *I'll* get in touch with you as to when I'll be available."

"Yes, Your Highness." Molly smirked, replacing the receiver. Then she made her way to Matt's office. Rapping lightly on his closed door, her insides churning, Molly could hear the sound of giggling coming from inside. Matt was not alone.

Suddenly, footsteps moved toward the door. Molly beat a hasty retreat to the nearest cover: a large fichus tree next to the water cooler. Peering between the leaves, Molly prayed that her green shirt would provide enough camouflage to avoid being spotted by Matt and his visitor.

Still giggling, a young, long-legged blonde stepped out of Matt's office with a smile on her full lips. She wore a pewter blouse in shimmering silk tucked into a short, brown suede skirt. High heels that came to a sharp point at the toe accentuated her trim legs. Her body was long, lean, and sinewy. She was like a beautiful blonde lioness. Swinging her long mane flirtatiously over one shoulder, she turned back to Matt and laid a graceful hand on his shoulder.

"You and I make such a great team," she purred.

Matt's cheeks reddened as he agreed. "I'm glad you had a chance to stop in today."

"Me too!" Blondie oozed, leaning into Matt's chest a little.

"Well, um . . ." Matt stammered, looking exactly as he had when Molly suggested they have dinner together the other night. What a fool she had been! Did he perform his Mr. Shy routine on all women?

"Well nothing, darling." Blondie gave him a playful poke in the chest. "I'll see you tonight. Bye for now." She turned and sashayed down the hallway.

Matt stood rooted to the floor, watching the sultry figure sway away. Molly caught a whiff of a strong, citrus-scented perfume. Who was that woman? Was Matt dating someone after all? From the way they'd been talking to each other, they obviously weren't strangers. Molly felt crushed. She could never hope to compete with someone who had the body of a Barbie doll and the fashion sense of Audrey Hepburn. Even the woman's heady perfume created a glamorous signature in the air around her.

Feeling she was going to be sick from the overwhelming scent and her own humiliation, Molly waited until Matt went back inside his office and closed the door behind him. Then she moved out from her hiding place, took a deep drink from the tepid water cooler, and fled.

Chapter 10

The kiln is a constantly changing personality, from the lag/quiet beginning to the dramatic climax of full fire, flame issuing from all ports, and greedy demands for fuel.
—Harry Memmott, from *Discovering Pottery*

Molly woke the next morning hoping that the sultry figure she had seen yesterday had belonged to a dream. Surely, that long-legged sex goddess wasn't Matt's girlfriend. Walking blearily into the bathroom, Molly turned on the shower and took a hesitant look in the steamy mirror. She examined her curvy, big-boned body and compared herself to the thin, lithe blonde. She felt totally depressed.

"Apples and oranges," she muttered to her foggy reflection. "No, not even. More like celery and pears."

Molly dressed in loose, comfortable clothes, stuck her hair in a ponytail, and went downstairs to eat breakfast.

The kitchen was strategically bare of comfort food, so she absently chewed on some nutritious cereal that was strongly reminiscent of the mulch she had recently put down around her bed of daylilies. Her sweltering car and an accident blocking both lanes leading to the office did nothing to improve her sour mood.

At work she sat listlessly at her desk and avoided looking in Matt's direction. It didn't take much of a sleuth to see how dejected she was, and when Clayton sat down opposite her later in the break room, he wasted no time in bringing up Matt.

"I can tell you saw our boy with that vixen yesterday," Clayton began, grimacing as he struggled with the wrapper of a banana MoonPie. "Did you smell that perfume? Ugh! Eau Du Tramp."

Molly smiled despite herself. "It was awfully musky, but she's still a stunning woman."

"Sure, if you like giggling twigs who smell like the cosmetic counter at JC Penny," Clayton said, closing his fingers over his nostrils as if the scent was still present.

"Do you think she's Matt's girlfriend?"

"I didn't think he had one and I know *everything* about *everyone's* love life." Clayton paused to think, his forefinger tugging at his bottom lip. "Still, I can find out."

"How?" Molly asked cautiously.

Clayton took a dainty bite out of his MoonPie and dusted a smattering of crumbs from his shirt as if each one were a poisonous insect. "He's got an appointment book. If she was his girlfriend he won't have her written in. Heaven forbid if she is! I will have totally misjudged the man for having good taste. Or," he taunted, "I could just ask him."

"No!" Molly started. "Don't do that. He'll guess I put you up to it."

"Honey, you just leave it all to little ole Clayton. I'm not the Queen Bee around here for nothing. Go get yourself busy with your next scintillating article and I'll be in touch." Clayton winked and blew her a theatrical kiss as he walked out of the room.

As she was ahead of schedule at work, Molly decided to shut down her computer and spend the rest of the day at home in her sweatpants, napping with her cats. Swanson was out, no doubt enjoying the fine weather by playing eighteen holes of golf, so there was no one to question her absence.

Her late afternoon snooze session on the deck surrounded by birdsong and perky geraniums in terra-cotta pots was interrupted by a call from her mother. "Why aren't you at Lex's preview party?" she demanded.

Molly plucked a red gummy bear from its bag underneath her plastic chaise and dropped it into her mouth. "Because," she said, chewing, "I'll see all those people tomorrow."

"But you always go when you're covering an auction. And we managed to work a dozen of George-Bradley's best pieces into tomorrow's sale by making an addendum to the catalogue. It's mobbed here already. So why aren't you coming?"

Molly hesitated. She was upset about the discovery of Matt's possible girlfriend, but she also didn't feel like getting dressed up in order to talk shop. She felt like an evening of TV, her two cats snuggled like bookends on her sofa, and a good sulk.

"I'm just tired," Molly told her mother.

"Fine. Listen, there's another reason I'm calling. I heard something on the radio today about Hillary Keane. Apparently he's been *found*, whatever that means. I couldn't hear anything else because Lex was on the cell phone extolling the virtues of an empire chest to a client. I did hear that there's going to be a report on the six o'clock news. I thought you'd be interested."

"He's been found?" Molly asked in wonder, the candy on her palm forgotten. "As in his *body* or as in discovered holed up in some seedy motel room with two kilos of coke?"

"I don't know. In between all the descriptions of the carvings and the details of the chest's provenance all I heard was Hillary's name and full details at six. You'd better watch," Clara said.

"Wow! Listen, I have to tell you what I discovered about him when I stopped by the pharmacy." Molly quickly filled Clara in on her conversation with Brandy. "I am going to be glued to that TV tonight, aren't you?"

"No. I came over to the gallery early to give the boys some directions for tomorrow. I'm running the floor and that means it's my responsibility to make sure they hold up the one-drawer stand instead of the umbrella stand during the sale. Lex couldn't have hired people who knew less about antiques if he picked them blindfolded."

Molly laughed, imagining her mother henpecking the four young men employed to haul furniture during sales. True, they weren't the sharpest tools in the shed, but at least they were capable of carrying huge wardrobes and heavy chests of drawers to people's cars. Those old pieces of furniture were solid masses of wood, awkward to carry and even harder to cram into backs of minivans and SUVs.

"Their lack of knowledge gives you the opportunity to educate them about the world of antiques. A world that's very important to a group of teenage boys," she teased her mother, feeling revived by the news about Keane. "Not only that, but you are a natural at bossing people around."

"Hmph," Clara snorted. "Any more educational opportunities and I'll be starting my cocktail hour right after lunch. 'Night, dear."

Molly stretched out on the couch and leafed through an antiques magazine while she waited for the news to come on. She mulled over her motives for not attending the preview. Normally, she lined up a future interview during this time—someone she was sure would spend a lot of money at the auction the following day. Now, she would have to cover the auction and acquire an interview candidate at the same time.

She admitted to herself that another reason for avoiding the party was that she hoped to receive a phone call from Clayton.

Popping several more candies in her mouth, she switched to the local news. The leadoff story concerned a national kidnapping case that, for once, had resulted in a happy ending. The little girl who had been taken to an abandoned house and tied to a pipe with duct tape had chewed through the tape and shouted for help from a broken window. The footage showed her safely at home with her parents and grandmother, being hugged tightly and given flowers and plush animals from the neighbors.

Molly was pleasantly surprised to see a positive story leading off the nightly news. She never watched it anymore because the focus of every piece was celebrity gossip, a grisly crime, or a political scandal. After a teaser about a possible baseball strike and a long commercial break, the anchorwoman lifted her shiny crown of platinum blonde hair and announced the capture of an antiquities thief in the western part of the state.

"This afternoon in Hendersonville," she intoned in a voice of dried-up honey, "authorities arrested forty-four-year-old Hillary Keane on charges of theft and driving under the influence. Sources say Keane swerved off the road, nearly hitting a jogger, before colliding with the guardrail and coming to a stop. Here's Phil with more."

The screen switched to a mountain road winding its way through a small town. The reporter, frowning in well-rehearsed consternation, stood before a curve in the road where the guardrail had buckled beneath the weight of Keane's van. The van was being removed on a flatbed tow truck behind Phil as he gave his report:

"This is the scene of what could have been a serious tragedy. Hillary Keane, a pharmacist from Asheboro, was swerving all over this twisted stretch of road when he almost hit Hendersonville's Clyde Farmer. Farmer was out jogging, hoping to get in a midday run before heading back to work at the post office. He almost didn't make it. When he saw Keane's oncoming vehicle, Farmer leapt over the guardrail in an attempt to avoid the oncoming car. He missed being hit by a matter of seconds. Farmer suffered minor injuries from his fall and is being treated at the local hospital."

Phil gestured at the guardrail and continued, "As if driving under the influence weren't enough, Keane is in even more hot water. Authorities report that several bins of stolen pottery were found in his battered vehicle. The pieces belong to different collectors across the state and are thought to be extremely valuable. Keane admitted that he was planning to sell them to an unknown buyer from Pennsylvania. Fortunately, none of the valuables were damaged in the crash. Authorities are *now* trying to discover who *else* was involved in the resale of the stolen goods. Keane is currently being held without bail. This is his second offense for driving while impaired." Phil produced a judgmental frown. "Marion, back to you."

"Hmm." Marion shook her shingled hair in disdain. "Looks like *someone* has a lot of explaining to do. Thanks, Phil. Up next, a Raleigh man gains much more than a pet when he visits his local animal shelter. Stay with us."

As the commercial break began, Molly frantically dialed the number to Lex's gallery. When Kitty answered, she asked her to fetch Clara to the phone right away.

"What's going on?" Kitty asked.

"Mom will tell you, just find her!"

When Clara heard the news, she was astounded. "A thief! I never would have guessed. I've seen him at sales for years. He seemed like a complete gentleman."

"I think he was to some people." Molly told Clara about the girl Keane had helped at the pharmacy. "Still, I bet Keane was stealing George-Bradley's pottery and he was found out. And now we know that he had a prior conviction for drunk driving. He probably had a hell of a time driving with those hands even when he was sober. Do you know what I'm thinking?"

"You still believe there's a connection to George-Bradley's death?"

"Maybe he just supplied the insulin. With such advanced rheumatoid arthritis, I don't think it's possible for him to have directly given George-Bradley the shot, but he's still a shady character."

Clara paused. "Keane was after pottery. He was greedy, but I don't see him aiding a killer. And why help someone kill George-Bradley now? Who else would benefit from his death?" Molly heard a crash in the background. "Listen, I can't think about all this detective stuff right now. I've still got so much to do here and Tweedledee and Tweedledum aren't getting any smarter."

Molly grinned. "I assume those are your new helpers. How's the crowd?"

"It's been super-busy. This should be a terrific sale. Lex is going to rake it in."

"Good for him. He works so hard for it."

"So do I!" Clara pretended to be hurt.

"And you do, too, Ma. See you in the morning."

• • •

Molly cooked chicken in a creamy mustard sauce for dinner and then watched the ten o'clock news to see if there were any more updates on Keane. What had that man been thinking? Why was he so desperate to sell the pottery that he stole from other collectors? Did he only steal from people he disliked as a kind of revenge? Was he an accessory to murder as well as a thief and a drunk? Maybe the girl in the pharmacy was covering for him. She obviously cared for him deeply, so she'd gladly give him an alibi.

Turning down her bedsheets, Molly stroked Griffin's soft brown and black fur as he curled up next to her. If Keane was guilty of being an accessory, she was sure the police would follow the trail created by the stolen pottery.

Inevitably, that trail would lead them to George-Bradley's house, where they would learn about his friendship with Keane from Bunny. Next, they would link the day of George-Bradley's death with Keane's sudden exodus. They would interview people who knew both men, and someone like Donald would tell them about the night George-Bradley called his former friend a thief. Linking all these clues together, the police would realize this was not a case of accidental death. They would ferret out the truth about Keane and question him about the person he had helped murder, a man no one seemed to miss.

Satisfied that the mysterious death of the infamous pottery collector was about to be solved by capable professionals, Molly drifted off to sleep.

Chapter 11

People need pots. You can see that from the way they love to look at them, to handle and to buy.
——Rosemary Zorza, from *Pottery: Creating with Clay*

A low fog hung out the window, holding the humidity hostage. Blades of grass reached wearily upward as dewdrops weighed down their yellow-green ridges. It was early. Even the birds were silent. No cars passed by, lawn mowers rested in their sheds, and children were still turning in their sleep, dreaming of triple-decker ice cream cones and riding their bikes to the pool, where they would find the courage to dive off the high board.

Molly's alarm pierced the tranquility with the high shrill of a Victorian policeman's whistle. Her cats remained immobile on the bed, their eyes closed in tight slits as they burrowed farther into their own feathery stomachs and ignored her movements as she shuffled downstairs to make coffee.

Once she reached Lex's gallery, she noticed that the parking lot was awfully full for an auction that didn't begin for another two hours. Before the sale started, Molly typically photographed the items she believed would bring the highest prices, but today she could see this might prove difficult if mobs of people were trying to preview pieces before the sale.

Clara agreed it would be a challenge. "I told you to come last night!" She scolded her daughter from her position behind the checkout counter. "How are you going to take pictures with all these people around?"

"I'll manage." Molly smiled at the signs of her mother's unusual nervousness, watching as she scanned her notes in the catalogue. Molly knew that organized, capable Clara had the location of every item memorized and could run the sale in her sleep, but her mother still worried. "Some courteous use of good manners is all it'll take. People won't mind standing aside for a few seconds. Don't worry, Ma, it's going to be a great sale."

Clara closed her catalogue and frowned. "I don't know," she said gloomily. "I woke up with this bad feeling that something was going to go wrong today."

Molly did not dismiss her mother's instinctual feelings—like her own, they had too often proved correct.

"Like what? Lex has obviously gotten a great deal of interest. I looked at the Internet bids last night and many things have already reached their estimates and the sale hasn't even begun."

Clara lowered her voice. "It's not the prices. It's something else."

"You didn't say anything to Lex about your vibe, did you?" Molly asked.

"Of course not." Her mother gestured to where Lex stood chatting up one of his frequent buyers. "He's already got a fever."

"Not again!" Molly couldn't help grinning. Lex habitually ran fevers before one of his quarterly sales. These were the ones that brought in the real profits for him. His weekly sales just paid the rent, and since he and Kitty were dreaming of buying a new home, this sale was especially important.

Molly watched him pat his forehead with a handkerchief before moving on to refocus the projection screen. Lex also hired people to hold the smaller items aloft so the crowd could view them with ease. After they were sold, the items were brought to a cordoned off holding area, where they were later packed and given over to their new owners only after a receipt was presented.

Between the Internet bidding and the live bids, Lex needed a large crew to run one of his premier sales, and though Molly enjoyed working the sales as much as Clara did, she found she could not glean the details she needed for her *Collector's Weekly* article while dashing to and fro looking for a snuffbox or a set of sterling spoons to hold up for the crowd.

Inside the main room, groups of buyers clustered before the display cases, carefully examining the selections of Southern pottery, some of which were from George-Bradley's collection. A sign taped to the sliding glass doors read, *Please do not handle the pottery. Ask for Assistance.* It was being completely ignored as collectors and dealers raised pieces out to the light, searching for minute cracks or flakes to the rims.

They swiveled jugs upside down, looking for the potter's stamp or a date. Each did their best to appear disinterested in the piece they examined, setting their faces into ambivalent masks as they ran their fervent fingers over the curves of clay. It was always the hands that gave their desire away.

Molly spotted Donald scrutinizing a pottery poodle glazed in earth brown. She watched Donald's face as he angled the piece and bobbed his head up and down so that his bifocal glasses could absorb all the details. Brows knit in concentration, he replaced the handsome poodle in its case and made a note in his sale catalogue. He liked the piece.

"Are you planning on buying up the whole showcase?" Molly greeted him with a teasing pat on the arm.

"Hello!" Donald hugged her warmly. "I might not be able to afford the prices today, but that N. Fox jug in the third case is a keeper." He glanced worriedly at the stream of incoming buyers, more of whom were filtering wide-eyed into the room like fish released into the open sea.

"Looks like a lot of people waited to preview until today," Molly said, following his gaze.

"It sure does," Donald agreed. "I came on Monday night so I could take a long look in private. It's good to have a friend *inside*"—Donald nodded in acquiescence in Clara's direction—"but I still like to get here early and get my seat."

Molly looked over at the end of the first row and saw Donald's name taped to a chair.

"I'd better snap photos of some of these pieces before the

showcases get too mobbed again." She excused herself and got to work taking photographs of the items she expected to fetch the highest prices.

It was almost impossible to interview bidders before a sale. They were too preoccupied and reluctant to say anything that could indicate their preferences. Molly focused on taking all the photos she could, then ambled over to the front desk, where Kitty was registering bidders and handing out reserved seating cards.

"Hey, Kitty." Molly greeted her friend with a quick hug. "Is it going to be a full house?"

"And then some," her friend said as she patted the pile of bidder numbers. They were already up over the hundreds. "We had to rent extra chairs, and people will still be standing."

Lex came over in search of his absentee bid sheets, his eyes darting about without settling on anything. Kitty placed an arm on his chest and handed him a bottle of water and three aspirin.

"You burning hunk of man, take these and I'll get you the sheets. I know exactly where they are."

Lex kissed her cheek and downed the aspirin. Molly got some short quotes on his feelings about the prime pieces in the sale, but then he was hailed by several prospective buyers and had no more time for chatting.

"We've got a problem," Clara said gravely as she appeared from the back room, holding one of the cordless phones in her hand. "Wade just called. Craven threw his back out last night and neither of them is coming! What are we going to do?"

Wade and Craven were experienced auction workers. They could lift the heaviest pieces of furniture without breaking a sweat and courteously help customers load their goods at the end of each sale.

Molly looked at her watch. It was nine thirty and the auction was scheduled to begin in thirty minutes. Two of the four men had called out sick. The other two were new and would be scrambling to move and locate all of the furniture during the sale. Also, there was so much pottery to be displayed, taken to the back, and carefully wrapped without damage. It was a serious problem.

"I don't think Will and Mike can handle the whole job!" Kitty wailed dramatically in between chewing on her nails. "They are too green!"

"They don't have any choice!" Clara snapped. "Today is the day Will learns what a mantel is." And she hurried off to find her victims.

Just then, Will shuffled in and grabbed a soda off the patrons' buffet table. Clara appeared with hands on hips, a clear sign that she was unhappy. "What kind of outfit is that for working a sale?"

Will's cap covered his eyes completely, and he had to peek out from under its brim to read the listing. As he snaked away from Clara's glare in order to review the listing of furniture he was to move, Molly noticed an odd shadowing on his skin. Browns, greens, and blues swirled around his eyes like smudges of paint. The left side of his lower lip was bloated and hung slightly forward, and a small cut worked its way through his upper chin.

"What happened to you?" Molly asked in concern. She didn't really know Will or Mike well as they were relatively new crewmembers, but she was shocked into bluntness by the sight of his bruises.

"Got in a fight," Will mumbled, a gleam of pride in his sunken eyes.

"When? Last night?" Molly couldn't believe he had been out carousing the night before one of the big sales.

"Nah, Thursday," Will said nonchalantly and walked off.

"Looks like you lost!" a bent old lady who was a regular buyer called after him, cackling maliciously.

Finally, it was time for the auction to begin. The last stragglers took their seats while those who were too edgy to sit found places to stand behind the back rows. Lex came to the podium to make his opening announcements. Molly winked encouragingly at Clara as her mother surveyed the crowd, her crew poised to begin the frantic pace.

From his elevated platform, Lex reminded the crowd that all of the items had been available to preview for over a week and that all purchases were final. Most of the audience talked through his opening speech, having heard it all a dozen times before.

"And lastly, thank you all for coming. Let's get started, shall we? Lot One. We have a fine gentleman's shaving stand made out of cherry. Excellent patina on this early piece. Let's start it off at one hundred dollars. Now one fifty. Now two hundred. Thank you."

Just as the item closed at a selling price of seven hundred fifty dollars plus buyer's premium, the power went off. The lights winked out and the humming computers went silent. The projection screen turned black and the air-conditioning ceased flowing through the vents. The crowd sat agog for a fraction of a second before turning about in their chairs and twittering animatedly with their neighbors.

Lex was frozen at the podium, but as he blinked his eyes and began to step down, the power snapped back on. He wiped his forehead in a dramatic gesture of relief and the crowd laughed.

"Can you reboot?" he called over to the two girls running the computers.

"Yeah, just give us a minute."

While Lex entertained the crowd with a story about another auction disaster, the computers were brought back to life and the image of Lot Two, a painted humidor, leapt onto the projection screen. Molly looked at her mother, whose mouth was set in a thin line of concern. Was this the event she had had a premonition about?

Then, Mike, the other new crewmember, pushed past Molly's seat in order to retrieve a cast-iron urn placed in a far corner. She recoiled at the strong smell of stale beer and cigarette smoke that hung in a tight cloud around his body. She also noticed that he bent to pick up a pottery jardinière instead of the iron urn.

"No, not that one," she whispered to him, pointing to the correct piece, "that one in the corner."

He turned to thank her, his eyes bloodshot and puffy with fatigue.

As she watched him reach out to grasp the urn, she saw that his hands were shaking. He was certainly not in a good state to be carrying valuable antiques. As he moved to grab the urn by its rim, she leaned over again, turning her nose away from his barroom odor.

"Grab it by the handles or the base. You'll drop it that way," she scolded. "And you'd better drink some water."

If Lex had any idea Mike was still inebriated on the day of his big sale, he would burst, but that reaction was nothing compared to the wrath Mike would face from Clara should he disturb the flow of the sale. With the veteran workers absent, Molly could see that the expectations set for Mike and Will were just too high. She was torn between sympathy and disgust for the irresponsible boys.

When Clara next came her way, loading her hands with two crystal decanters, Molly warned her of potential disasters.

"Mike's got a nasty hangover," she whispered.

"Hangover? The boy is dead drunk!" Clara retorted and whisked her items up to the front.

Twenty lots later, Mike was nowhere in sight.

"Molly." Kitty appeared at her side, gripping her arm like a vise. "Mike left. He just left!"

"What?" Molly asked, astounded.

Kitty whispered urgently, "He left! He said he was peeing blood and had to go to the hospital."

Molly looked across the room at her mother, who was scrambling to prepare a table full of pottery to be auctioned off in the next few minutes. "Oh, Lord."

"You've got to get up there! Your mom can't handle all this," Kitty pleaded.

Molly left her notepad on her chair and wove her way around the standing observers until she reached the front. She whispered the dire news to Clara, who unhesitatingly shoved a catalogue in her hands.

"I *told* you something bad was going to happen. Still, I'd rather have you up here anyway. You're now in charge of all the pottery. I'll grab you if we need to lift something small. Otherwise, we're going to have to use the wand."

The wand was a stick with a star glued to its tip that the crew used to point to objects that were just too bulky to bring up front for the crowd to view.

"We have the projection screen, too," Molly reminded her mother. "They'll know what we're selling." And she quickly grabbed the next lot, a pottery lamb, and held it aloft before the audience.

Lex did a double take when he saw her, but didn't miss a beat of his selling lilt. As he opened the bidding, Molly watched the same old lady who had cackled at Will hold her bidder number firmly in the air. Donald raised his as well, and it came down to just the two of them fighting for the pottery animal. Finally, Donald shook his head and looked back down at his lap, a sign that he was done bidding. The old woman lifted her face and smiled with pleasure.

"That lady is having a ball," Molly whispered.

"I'm glad *someone* is," Clara returned, waving for Will to pick up the next lot.

As Molly watched him carry a Persian runner up to the front, her eyes fell on a familiar puff of hair in the audience.

Bunny Staunton was seated in the third row. She had never come to one of Lex's sales before, but since some of her late husband's pottery was about to be sold, she probably wanted to bear witness to its true value. Catching Molly's eye, she gave a cursory nod of recognition, then turned her gaze to the next lot, the first of her husband's collection.

The piece, a Ben Owen two-handled tapered vase glazed in Chinese blue with large patches of red, was an extremely handsome item. The large amount of red glaze seeping through like a sunrise would raise the price, and bidding cards flapped around the room like white wings, eager to be spotted.

Finally, the last two bidders battled it out. One was a man seated toward the back wearing jeans and a faded flannel shirt. Molly knew, despite his casual dress, that he was quite wealthy and was a fervent pottery collector as well. She craned her neck to catch a view of the second bidder and instantly recognized the neat, trim figure wearing a silk blouse and a double strand of pearls. It was Susan, George-Bradley's former mistress.

She sat on the opposite side of the room from Bunny, about two rows back. She could observe Mrs. Staunton, but Bunny couldn't see her. Susan's lips, shiny with a trendy gloss, were pursed in dogged determination as she won the lot. She made a notation in her catalogue and prepared to bid on the next. As each piece of George-Bradley's collection came up for sale, she waged a relentless war against other bidders until she laid claim to the majority of his better pieces.

Soon, several people turned to see who the persistent buyer was, including a disgruntled Donald. Even Bunny was curious, and she turned to look behind her shoulder just as a large C.C. Burle devil face jug came up for sale. It was the very piece Susan and George-Bradley had wrestled over at the kiln opening. Susan sat erect in her chair, raising her bidding card with delicate flicks of her tiny wrist.

From her vantage point, Molly could see the two women clearly. As she held up an unsigned whiskey jug for the audience to view, she watched Bunny discover the identity of the determined bidder.

Susan glanced over at Bunny, her bidding card held up like a shield.

The two women locked eyes, but only for a moment, exchanging looks of venomous loathing before Bunny sneered in disdain and turned back around. Molly could see that underneath her thick makeup and attempts to control her expression, Bunny's eyes were filled with a cold rage. She looked down at her catalogue, cheeks flushed with anger and humiliation.

"Poor Bunny," Molly whispered to Clara, as mother and daughter witnessed the other woman's misery.

Clara, who never missed a single detail of the entire sale, handed Molly an antique Cherokee basket. "This is next. And yes, I feel bad for her too."

For Bunny, this should have been a moment of triumph. Like the photographs in her home, Bunny had appeared at the sale as the devoted wife of the late George-Bradley Staunton. Everyone attending the auction knew who she was and had paid their respects to her over the loss of her husband and had extolled the virtues of his collection. If his pottery sold well, it only increased her husband's reputation as a collector and made it easier to maintain her illusion of having married a well-known man with impeccable taste. The presence of her husband's former mistress evaporated that image into mist.

As the last of George-Bradley's pottery sold, Bunny made her way to the restroom. When she returned, she passed right by the row where her reserved seat was located and crossed into the front room. Through the window, Molly saw her open the door to her silver BMW and sit down inside without starting the ignition.

Unable to pay any more attention to Bunny, Molly and Clara worked like frenzied bees for the next two hours. In between lots, they guzzled water and took hasty bites of ham and cheese sandwiches. By the last lot, they were dead on their feet.

As buyers lined up to pay Kitty for their items Lex asked, "Can one of you guys help wrap some pottery?" He was still ignorant of what the three of them had accomplished without Mike's help.

"No," Clara said wearily. "The customers can wrap their own. We've had it."

"Where's Mike?" Lex looked around.

Clara filled Lex in on the details of Mike's departure as Molly moved her leaden legs down to the wrapping area to assist with the pottery. Of course it was Susan's huge pile that required so much attention, but Lex was almost out of boxes.

"Do you have anything to pack these in?" she asked Susan with as much politeness as she could muster.

"I might have some bins in my car," she replied haughtily. "But I would expect you to provide boxes since I'm spending all this money."

"I'll come out with you to fetch them," Molly offered reluctantly, her fatigue and dislike for the petite woman causing her to wish she had not volunteered to help. She wondered if Susan would be embarrassed about being so snotty when Molly showed up on her doorstep a few days later for their interview. Right now, Susan thought Molly was simply another member of Lex's crew, unworthy of cordiality.

"Oh, fine, let's go," Susan drawled. "But hurry up, I don't have all day."

Susan's white Mercedes SUV looked brand new. Molly wondered what Susan did for a living to be able to afford such an expensive car and lot after lot of costly pottery. Her car retailed for around eighty grand, and she had probably spent ten thousand at today's sale. All of her clothes were designer labels and her shoes alone were the latest fashion of monogrammed leather that cost three hundred dollars a pair.

As Molly climbed into the back of the car to dig out plastic bins, Bunny suddenly appeared at Susan's side. Inside the SUV, Molly pivoted her body to watch as Bunny raised her hand and pointed a shiny, manicured talon at Susan's chest.

"How dare you!" Bunny breathed heavily. "How dare you show up here and bid on *my* husband's things!"

Susan was completely unruffled. She looked Bunny up and down in disgust and shook her coiffed crown of hair. "Last time I checked, this was a *public* auction."

"You piece of trash. I know where you came from. People like you never shake off the trailer park dirt, no matter what you drive or wear." Bunny waved at Susan's clothes in dismissal.

Through the open car door, Molly could see the heat rise in Susan's face. The "trailer park" comment had hit home.

"Your husband didn't seem to mind," Susan retorted in a low, taunting voice. Then she ran her hands over her small hips and smiled evilly.

Bunny looked as if an arrow had struck her straight through the heart. Molly was afraid that the malicious look on Bunny's face meant she was about to do something rash. Instead, she simply hissed, "You were just another *thing* he collected!"

Turning away, Bunny seemed to think of one more verbal dagger she could thrust into Susan. "By the way," she said, turning back to Susan and grinning slyly, "my lawyer paid me a visit this week. You know, to review *my* husband's estate. He gave me a sealed letter that George-Bradley had left for me to read in the event he should die before me. I found it most interesting. Do you want to know what it said?"

Susan stood silently, her face empty of expression. She looked as though she had forgotten how to breathe.

And then, leaning in as if she were going to kiss Susan on the cheek, Bunny began whispering something into her ear. Molly brazenly scooted over the warm surface of Susan's leather seat in order to get closer to the open door, but the only thing she was able to catch was "your little car ride in the backwoods that day."

Susan's face, which had been screwed up in anger, rapidly blanched chalk white and her eyes grew round in shock. She stood rooted to the ground, fists clenched at her sides like a hoplite statue. All the fight was gone from her. Triumphant, Bunny walked away, slowly and with careful dignity. Molly saw her opportunity to leave, grabbed her bins as quietly as possible, and scurried back to the gallery.

As she watched Susan drive off with all her pottery left behind, Clara came to stand beside her.

"Susan left without her pottery!" Clara exclaimed. Sinking down into the nearest chair, she mused tiredly, "Who won *that* fight, I wonder."

Molly thought about the circumstances that had driven the opposing women together. Bunny was now a widow, desperately trying to hold on to her public image as George-Bradley's happy wife. Susan, whose passion for pottery had once united her with the same man, now sought to buy all the pieces George-Bradley had owned.

Somehow, Susan's relationship with George-Bradley had soured. They had become rivals, fighting over pottery at C.C.'s kiln opening like two children squabbling over a toy in the playground.

What had Bunny whispered about a "car ride" to elicit such a powerful reaction? It must have meant something awful to Susan to make her leave behind thousands of dollars of pottery, even temporarily.

Molly sighed, thinking about her first impression of George-Bradley. He had been rude, lecherous, and greedy. Why would any woman fight over a man like him?

She shrugged. "No one won, Ma. In fact, I think that was just Round One."

Chapter 12

Pottery making is a discipline that, once one is thoroughly hooked, is like an addiction and almost impossible to separate from.
—Robin Hopper, from *Functional Pottery Form and Aesthetic in Pots of Purpose*

L ate that afternoon, Molly reviewed the notecards scattered in an arc across her desk space. After carefully forming the outline for her next article, she planned to go home and spend the rest of the day reading out on her cozy deck. "Hello, love." Clayton stood before her wearing a pink and blue striped shirt and designer jeans with cowboy boots.

"You always look so good, Clayton."

"Honey, you look like last week's wash. Look at your nails. You have been terribly negligent of those cuticles," Clayton admonished her. "I believe a spa day is in order."

"Doesn't anyone take a day off around here?" Molly asked testily.

"Temper, temper. I just sashayed over to share some exciting news about that Keane fellow. See, I was having a lovely phone conversation with darling Francis over at the *Sun Times* and oh, that boy has the face of an—"

"Clayton! Don't be a tease," Molly interrupted him.

Clayton sulked. He liked to build up his story before getting to the good bits of gossip.

"All right, I'm sorry. Tell me about Keane now and then you can go into minute detail about Francis and his many attractions over a cappuccino after work. My treat," added Molly.

Clayton relented. "Yummy. And since I can't resist your wide-eyed pleading look, it's a deal. So! It seems that Keane got his liquor on pretty early the day he nearly hit that jogger. Started out at a truck stop, where he was giving a little lift to his coffee out of a flask. From there, he ended up drinking beer at some pool hall that calls itself a restaurant. Heading back to his seedy motel, where he'd been holed up for the last week, he almost hit that marathon man." Clayton grimaced in distaste. "I mean, sweet Jesus, who stays in a motel anymore? Hello? Book a hotel, with an *h*."

"Was this seedy motel in Asheboro?"

Clayton paused to think. "No. Just outside Hendersonville. The waitresses at the truck stop all remembered him because he came in every morning to drink coffee laced with bourbon. Thing is, the little dear could never get the cap back on his bourbon flask. Bad case of the shakes, I guess."

"Not exactly," Molly said. "Keane was acting like a guilty man who happens to be afflicted with rheumatoid arthritis. He may have stolen pottery, but now I know he couldn't have killed George-Bradley. It's a wonder he could drive at all with those hands."

Molly was finished viewing Keane as a murder suspect. Clara was right. Keane was interested in pottery, not violence. He was guilty of greed and a stringent case of envy, but Molly believed Bunny or Susan had given George-Bradley the extra dose of insulin. Poison was more of a woman's method anyway, and Molly considered an overdose just another means of poisoning the body.

Her thoughts turned back to the scene from the auction. She recalled Bunny's menacing whisper and Susan's shocked face. What else had George-Bradley written in that letter?

And the calm rage Bunny had exhibited was certainly a side of the widow that Molly hadn't guessed the older woman possessed. Bunny must have committed the murder. She was alone in the house with her husband and was the only other person who had access to his medicine. Of course she had wanted revenge. Her husband had made a fool of her for years. But why now? Molly needed to get into Bunny's house and find out more about George-Bradley's widow. It was time to arrange an interview with Mrs. Staunton.

"Miss Molly," Clayton interrupted her thoughts, "I do believe you haven't listened to a word I was saying. Let's go get that cappuccino and a manicure. I can see that you need a break."

"You're right. Let me just check my messages first. I forgot to listen to them yesterday."

There was only one new voice mail message. As Molly listened, a muffled voice began to speak in a near whisper. A flat, cold tone filled with malice hissed through the receiver. "Stay out of things that don't concern you," the voice threatened slowly. "Some stones are better left unturned. If you don't butt out, you'll be sorry. I'll be watching you." The message ended.

"Molly? Honey?" She heard Clayton's voice as if from a long way off.

She handed him the phone and replayed the message.

"Mother Mary and all the saints!" Clayton cried, dropping the phone as if it were on fire. His hands fluttered in the air like startled birds as he shrieked, "We've got to call the police!"

Clayton dialed and released a loud and frantic tirade to the unfortunate soul who answered the phone.

Wanting to avoid listening to the message again, Molly walked numbly to the ladies' room, where she splashed cold water on her face and tried to digest the threatening message. It had not sounded familiar; the voice was too muffled to be distinctive. She couldn't even tell if it had been a man or a woman. It had been recorded last night, but that meant nothing. She needed to sit down and think this through.

Who had she talked to about her theories? Only to people she knew well. So who had called her? Bunny? She had no idea Molly suspected her of murder. Susan? Could Susan have killed George-Bradley and Bunny had discovered proof within the letter? Was that the frightening secret Bunny had whispered in Susan's ear?

There were no clear answers and none of Molly's theories explained why she'd received the call last night.

Clayton suddenly interrupted her thoughts in his full dramatic glory. He flung open the restroom door with a cry and dragged her into the break room. Clucking like a mother hen, he plied Molly with coffee and a stale cheese Danish and wrung his hands over her until a policeman arrived.

Molly issued a brief statement, and though Clayton did his best to elevate the seriousness of the matter, the policeman didn't seem overwhelmingly concerned.

"Press people get anonymous threats all the time," he said flatly, removing one of Clayton's hands from his arm. "Usually not at newspapers writing articles on old stuff, but it happens. Just let me know if it you get another call." He turned to Molly, giving her his card. "Seems like it was from a throwaway cell phone, so we have no way to trace it. Probably some kid getting his kicks by crank calling people."

"Thanks," Molly mumbled, taking his card. She was relieved that she hadn't shared that the threatening call was undoubtedly related to George-Bradley's murder. The policeman would probably assume she was reading too many mysteries and was only looking for attention.

Clayton followed him out, gushing about the shock it had caused him. Molly heard a third voice enter the conversation as she stacked her index cards and packed her bag to go home. It was Matt's soft tenor coming from the lobby.

"Are you all right?" he said, appearing at her side, his face creased in concern.

Thinking back to his leggy blonde visitor, Molly replied without meeting his eyes. "Yes, I'm fine."

As she picked up her bag and moved to leave, Matt blocked her path. Startled, she looked up at him.

"Clayton told me what happened. He's a wreck, but I'm worried about you. Can't I do something?" he asked.

"No." Her voice softened. Matt really was a nice guy, even if he had a girlfriend. "Thank you, though."

"I don't think you should be alone tonight. Do you feel up to going out for dinner?"

"Can't. I already promised my mother I'd come over. And to be honest," Molly began, eyeing Matt shrewdly, "I'd like to go out to dinner with you, but I'm not sure that blonde I saw you with the other day would approve."

Matt looked confused, and then laughed aloud as if Molly had delivered the punch line to a great joke. "Amy? Amy Byrd? That was a business meeting. Amy's a rep for Grant's Auction House over in Wilson. They are going to start running full-page ads with the paper every week. She's not my girlfriend."

"Oh." Molly was embarrassed. "It's just that I heard her saying she'd see you later that night and I assumed . . ."

"We were both invited to a party for one of my med school friends. She's dating an old buddy of mine. I wish she wasn't dating him, though, because she's an awful flirt. But I'm not in the least bit attracted to her." He smiled at Molly. "I don't go in for stick figures."

"What a lovely thing to say, Matt Harrison." Molly was pleased. She forgot all about the intimidating message as she gazed into his twinkling blue eyes. "And just what is your type?" She was astonished by her boldness.

Matt opened his mouth and spoke as many words in one breath as she had heard him utter in the two years they'd worked for the same paper. "I like a woman with smarts. Someone with a good heart and a quick laugh. I like a woman to look like a woman. Someone who will eat dinner with you instead of pushing two pieces of lettuce around on her plate while she looks around to see who might be admiring her. I like a woman who believes in family, friends, and the American flag. A woman who has framed photos of her cats on her desk." Matt exhaled. He looked as surprised as Molly by the length of his monologue. "I like a woman like you. You're my type," he finished with a soft whisper and then leaned in to kiss her.

Chapter 13

Despite the falling rain and crackling of the flames, everyone heard the detonations . . . Generally it is the larger, thicker-walled wares that suffer the most; the smaller pots in the case showed no damage at all.
　　　　　　　—Charles G. Zug III, from *Turners and Burners*

Monday morning dawned at the Staunton Estate without its usual birdsong and squirrel chatter. Instead, a row of pickups and workmen in jeans broke the pastoral tranquility with the sharp staccato of hammering, the whine of handheld saws, and the crackling of snapping wood.

Two men in jeans and black T-shirts carried the massive shelves that once held George-Bradley's pottery collection outside. Handmade from solid walnut, they were both heavy and attractive, but Bunny told the foreman he could keep the whole lot.

"What's Walt gonna do with these?" one worker asked another.

"Use 'em," grunted the second beneath the weight of the shelves, "for books."

"Books?" The first man laughed as they slid the shelves onto the bed of one of the trucks.

"He's a Civil War buff, remember?"

The two men headed back inside. The oriental rugs in the main hall had been removed and sheets of plastic covered the hardwood floors. A thin layer of dust had already settled upon the sheet, and the buzz of power tools grew louder inside the wing where George-Bradley had once spent most of his free time.

Inside the music room, two men were ripping up the dark brown carpet and rolling it in wide strips to be hauled outside. In the office, the last of the shelves were being removed while two men stood over the massive mahogany desk and admired its waxy surface. The drawers were still stuffed with stationery, rubber bands, staples, and sundry supplies.

"Hey, chief!" one of the men called out.

A tall man wearing a short-sleeved, plaid button-down shirt stepped inside. He removed his John Deere baseball cap, wiped the sweat from his brow, and surveyed the room.

"What've you boys got?"

"What's the plan for this desk?"

The foreman, Walter Hogue, ran his calloused fingers over the leather and wood desktop. He understood, without being knowledgeable about antiques, that the piece had been made by hand. The workmanship was so fine that he had trouble finding the joinery.

"Hidden dovetails." He nodded in admiration. He stood and gestured outside. "Unfortunately, it goes out to the garage for now. The lady doesn't want anything left in this area."

"Just clear the whole place out, is that the plan?" one of the men asked.

"Yep. Seems the lady's sister is moving in and this is going to be her part of the house."

"Shoot, there's enough room upstairs to house the whole choir of Shady Grove Baptist, why go through all this renovation?"

Walt shrugged his wide, bony shoulders. "Don't know. Everyone needs their own space, I guess. Anyway, when the customers pay in cash, I don't ask too many questions."

"Well, it's her money." The two men strained under the weight of the desk and Walt jumped in to lend a hand.

Passing the library, he noticed the rest of his crew standing in a group before the wall facing the window.

"Y'all studying something?" he called out. "We're being paid to work, not to sightsee."

One of the workers pointed at the fine mahogany wall paneling with his sledgehammer. "Chief, are we really supposed to tear all this out?"

Another man lifted his crowbar. "It seems crazy to dig into this stuff. It must've cost a fortune. Are you sure she wants it all smashed to bits?"

Walt gazed around the room again. He had gone over every detail with Mrs. Staunton, making sure that he had a crystal-clear understanding of her instructions. Yet it wouldn't do to make a mistake when it came to such fine paneling. He had asked her the same question. Such excellent and costly workmanship—was she sure she wanted it removed? But Mrs. Staunton replied that she was positive. She'd even handed him a can of paint called perky periwinkle to use on the newly stripped walls.

"Look, boys, the lady said all this wood made the room too dark and too masculine for her sister, so she wants it out. We're painting these walls purple."

"Chief." The man with the sledgehammer shook his head solemnly. "It's a sheer crime, that's what it is."

"I know. Let me do the hard part for you." Walt grabbed the hammer and swung it into the nearest wood panel. A gaping hole of splintered wood appeared. He grabbed the edges around the hole and pulled, tearing out slices of wood and throwing them in the center of the room.

"Ouch," one of his men murmured, then dug his crowbar around the seams, splitting wood and popping out nails.

Walt returned the tool to its owner and pointed at the gaping rent in the polished paneling. "Spell's broken. Get going."

Shaking his head at the destruction of such a fine room, Walt returned to the garage, where other members of his crew had carried the desk. They stood beside it, smoking cigarettes and laughing. Walt was annoyed to find his workers idle.

"Waitin' on keys, chief," one of them quickly volunteered. "Door's locked."

The gardener appeared like Houdini from behind the garage, swinging a bundle of keys from a rope like a lifeguard. Walt had seen him when he'd visited the mansion to give Mrs. Staunton an estimate on the job. The gardener was a middle-aged Hispanic man with coffee-colored skin, wide dark eyes, and nut-brown hair. His face, although wrinkled prematurely by years of working in the sun, was handsome, and his eyes sparkled with intelligence and confidence.

"Looking for these?" he asked Walt in a deep, accented voice. Walt noticed that he was taller than he'd seemed from a distance and his arms were sinewy and thick with strength. He had the build of a much younger man. He smelled of rich soil and cut grass.

"Thank you . . ." Walt accepted the keys and struggled to remember the man's name.

"Emmanuel." The gardener smiled, displaying a row of well-shaped white teeth. Walt couldn't help but notice a smudge of pink lipstick on the gardener's chin. Emmanuel was fooling around with a lady in the house. As interesting as that fact may be, Walt knew that it was none of his business. He was here for a job and he needed to get back to it.

Opening the garage door, his crew shuffled inside with the desk and placed it against the back wall. Walt then rejoined his crew in the library, where the work on the paneling was going smoothly. A large scrap pile was building in the center of the room. Electrical lines wound like vines from ceiling to floor. He gestured to one of the men to hand over his crowbar.

"Get the wheelbarrow. We've got to clean some of this out of here."

The men worked quickly, joking with one another and sharing stories as they tore out the wood and piled pieces into the wheelbarrow. In the corner of the back wall, Walt dug his crowbar through the panel against the floor. The hooked end of his tool went deep behind the wood, meeting with no resistance. Surprised, Walt knelt and began prying the fractured wood away from the initial hole. Instead of seeing the same cracked wall behind the panel, a dark space peered back at him.

"Roy, hand me your flashlight."

"Sure, chief."

Walt stuck the small face of the flashlight into the hole and switched the light on. The beam fell onto a trio of white shoeboxes, nestled like sleeping geese on a pile of newspaper.

"What's that, chief? Secret hiding spot?"

Walt removed the flashlight and stood. "Yeah, I think so. I'd better get Mrs. Staunton. Don't touch anything."

Walt found Bunny outside, cutting plum-colored roses. She carried a wide, flat basket and hummed as she selected dozens of plump blooms for her arrangements. A large straw hat with a black ribbon masked her face.

"Ma'am?" Walt called as he approached her.

"Yes?" Bunny spoke without glancing away from her task.

"We've found something in your husband's . . . well, inside one of the walls."

Bunny looked at him in confusion. "*In* the wall?"

"I think you'd better come inside."

After a moment's pause, Bunny nodded and put her basket down. She followed Walt quietly into the library, where the noise had ceased and the men stood around in a cluster, waiting to see what would happen next.

Walt led Bunny to the hole in the back wall and handed her the flashlight. As she switched on the light, Walt ushered his men out of the room.

"Give her some privacy," he scolded. He was curious too, of course, but made it a rule not to get involved with his clients' personal business. If they wanted to have affairs with the gardener, fine. If they had stashes of drugs or cash hidden behind the wall, fine. As long as he did his job and got paid for it, the wealthy citizens of Asheboro could lead their eccentric lifestyles. Walt worked in construction, not in therapy or criminal justice. He knew when to make himself scarce.

"Come on, boys. Coffee break."

• • •

Bunny reached inside the hole and pulled out the three shoeboxes. She noticed a latch on the panel's frame, which must have served as the release button, though it was hidden to the naked eye. A person would only need to press the right place on the frame and the panel would pop open a crack. Hidden behind a large wingback chair, no one would have randomly bumped against the spot. No wonder Bunny hadn't been aware of the existence of a secret panel in her husband's study.

Her hand rested on the dusty lid of the first box. Bunny hesitated. Did she really want to know what was inside? She knew enough of her husband's sordid past as it was. What else was there to damage her memory of him? Illegitimate children? A secret will?

Bunny sighed, and for the millionth time thought about her life with George-Bradley when they had first been married. They had lived in a quaint cottage outside of town. She had grown vegetables in the small garden out back. He had practiced law and tinkered at his workbench, making wind chimes out of scrap metal. They ate watching television, drank lots of wine, and made love every night. When they moved into this house, bought with the money Bunny inherited from her parents, she thought she was living in a dream.

But the dream slowly faded. Unable to have children, Bunny began growing prize roses obsessively, and George-Bradley began collecting pottery. She took gourmet cooking classes but her husband was never home to eat her creations. She knew he was seeing other women, and her only comforts became the blue ribbons her roses won and the food she cooked. She put on weight; he stayed downstairs in his wing of the house until bedtime. When he finally got into bed, reeking of cigars and bourbon, he immediately turned away from her and went to sleep. Their only physical contact occurred when Bunny had the pleasure of jabbing her husband in the belly with a small needle twice a day. What had happened to their marriage?

Bunny looked at the gutted walls. The oldest of two children, Bunny had inherited a larger portion of her parents' estate. Her sister, Caroline, had money too, but she never spent any. A spinster, she was a teacher at the nearby middle school. Her retirement was coming up in a few months, and the two sisters decided to meet old age comfortably together in Bunny's house. Bunny wanted to create a separate apartment suite for her sister. She wanted it to be bright and cozy and feminine. No trace of her husband would remain.

There would be no more secrets in Bunny's life either. She would tell Caroline that she was in love with Emmanuel. Finally, she would surrender the sham that she had had the perfect marriage. She would drop the role of grieving widow and get rid of all those ridiculous photographs in the living room. People she actually cared about would be placed in those frames.

Taking in a deep breath that tasted of wood and dust, Bunny decided that her husband no longer had the power to hurt her. She popped off the lid of the first box. Inside were neat piles of bills, held together with rubber bands and covered in plastic wrap. Bunny saw that they were all stacks of hundreds. A few thousand dollars of ready cash. This was certainly a positive discovery.

Relieved, Bunny set the box aside and opened the second. Documents were rolled up neatly inside a plastic tube. Flattening them revealed a pile of bearer bonds, in denominations of ten thousand dollars. Bunny counted the bonds. A quarter of a million dollars' worth! Why had George-Bradley stashed away all this money? Perhaps he was planning to divorce her so he could get back together with Susan Black. Why else would he hide bonds in a secret panel?

Clutching the papers in anger, Bunny swore.

"He must have been stealing from our joint account for years! I'd kill that bastard myself if he wasn't already dead."

She stared at the third box.

"Now what, George-Bradley?" she asked the still air. "You haven't done enough to ruin my life?"

The third box revealed a solid, heavy lump wrapped in newspaper. Bunny broke through layers of tape and newspaper with her long, sharp nails. Unwrapping the object inside, she stared down at it, perplexed. This required further examination.

Gathering the boxes in her hands, she headed for her wing of the house, giving a brief nod in the foreman's direction to signal that she had completed her business. He immediately called his men back to work.

Safely in her study. Bunny dumped the boxes on her desk. After staring at the object in the third box for a long moment, she picked up the phone and began dialing.

"At least I know how to get rid of you. You aren't even glazed. Probably worth nothing, just like my jerk of a husband." She jabbed the object with a scarlet talon, and then turned her attention to the voice on the phone. "Lex Lewis, please."

• • •

Warmth and sunlight woke the clay. Even through the thick wrapping it could sense the power of release. The clay waited patiently while the folds of newspaper were removed from its curved body. It seemed like eons since its pores last breathed the moving air. Blinded by light, it lay impassive as it allowed the dust to swirl curiously around its form, settling into the round lines of its tail and between the nooks of its paws.

Nails scraped along its body, harshly scratching at its exposed skin, still fragile after so much time alone in the damp darkness.

The rabbit was turned upside down. Its ears hung above the ground, listening for the sound of the heavy footsteps of the man who had hidden him away. His scent lingered, but there were other, more recent smells too. The strong tinge of enamel paint, the rubbery smell of caulk, and a brush encrusted with polyurethane. Then there was the scent of the woman. Flowery and strong, it spoke to the clay of disguises. It shrank away from the nails and the chemical-tinged perfume, turning back to the fading memory of the potter's hands.

The clay was carried off irreverently on one of the woman's palms and then dumped onto the polished surface of a black lacquered desk. It listened to her voice, brittle and demanding, drift off to another place beyond the room.

"You're not even glazed," her cold voice judged the clay, turning it back and forth and upside down before dismissing it as an item of little worth.

The woman left, taking with her a cloud of anger and disappointment. The quiet crept in on light feet, settling around the clay and soothing it with gentle strokes of stillness and sunshine.

Outside, a few leaves drifted lazily onto the shady slopes of grass. A thin wisp of air carried a gift of magnolia blossoms and boxwoods to the clay. Yellow finches gathered near the west window, darting flashes of color before the clay's parched eyes. Calmed, it inhaled the summer, the season of its birth.

With the ancient knowledge of the stones and water that had come together to form its heart, the clay knew that someone was coming for it. Someone was coming, someone who had the right hands. Someone who recognized the spirit, the spark of life residing deep within the clay.

The potter was gone and the clay had been alone for a long time now. But soon, very soon, it would be given a home, and a place of honor among the other things birthed from wood and stone and earth. Soon.

The clay opened up its pores to capture the soft breath of wind seeping through the sills. It could wait here for a while. For now, no more darkness would follow.

Chapter 14

But we have this treasure in jars of clay to show that this all-surpassing power is from God and not from us.

—2 Corinthians 4:7

C lara called when Molly was in the middle of previewing items at Bud Earl's Auction Company in Greensboro. As a writer for *Collector's Weekly*, Molly was allowed a private preview. Lingering over a folk art painting of the Statue of Liberty, Molly was so captivated by the bright colors, polka dots, and stripes decorating the frame that it took her a minute to recognize that the annoying buzzing interrupting her concentration was coming from her purse.

"Hello?"

"Madam? Are you still at Earl's?" Clara asked.

"I am." Molly moved on to the next painting. It was a primitive work of an African-American man being chased by an oversized snake. Simply called *Black Snake* by the artist, it had been painted on a piece of pine that had once served as part of an outhouse door.

Yesterday's threatening voice mail had almost faded in light of the lively folk art and the warm memory of Matt's kiss, which she replayed in her mind again and again.

"He have anything good?" Clara broke into her daughter's reverie.

"Some great folk art," Molly reluctantly admitted. After all, other auction companies were direct competition for Lex.

"Can you do Lex and me a huge favor?" Clara asked.

"What is it?"

"Bunny found one more piece of George-Bradley's pottery. Would you mind picking it up? I've got an appraisal in Raleigh so I'm too busy to drive two hours the other way to fetch it."

Molly was a bit apprehensive about seeing Bunny after witnessing her face-off with Susan, and yet she was already halfway to Asheboro.

Not only that, but she could use this opportunity to dig more information up on the Staunton marriage and George-Bradley's last morning alive. Molly was certain she'd get some kind of vibe about whether or not Bunny was guilty of murder. Maybe she'd even learn more about the mysterious letter. "Sure," she told Clara charitably. "What is the piece?"

"Don't know, but Bunny said it wasn't glazed, so it's no keeper. We just want to keep her happy because she gave us George-Bradley's collection and she does travel in influential circles."

"Maybe I'll just offer her some cash for the piece," Molly joked. "Use it as a paperweight at work."

"Go right ahead. Lex doesn't even want it. It won't fit in with the rest of the collection we're auctioning next month. And after all the money we got for that woman for the first group, she didn't seem the least bit grateful."

Molly paused. "It's not the money, Ma. The pottery just held bad memories for her. She just wants to be done with it."

"As we want to be done with her. Thanks." Clara rang off.

Stuffing her phone back in her purse, Molly finished viewing the artwork. Earl had over two dozen primitive folk art paintings from a variety of North Carolina artists. Folk art was becoming a hot item across the East Coast and Molly had decided to write an introductory piece about folk art in addition to her article describing today's auction. She hoped Swanson would approve. Taking down some notes on several of the artists, she thanked the auctioneer and headed once more for Bunny's house.

• • •

After ringing the doorbell for the third time, Molly let out a sigh of frustration. Clearly, no one was going to answer. Through the front window, she could see a shoebox propped on the hall table with the words *Lex Lewis* marked on it. Boldly, Molly decided to try opening the door. To her surprise, it was unlocked.

Tiptoeing over to the small box stuffed with paper, Molly picked it up and carefully peeled back the folds of tissue. She saw the face of a clay rabbit peering up at her from its white nest. It had been fired, but never glazed.

The little rabbit, with its winking eyes and long, perky ears, smiled up at her. She delicately traced its incised whiskers and felt the curve of its graceful hind leg. She stroked the two front paws and ran her fingertips lovingly down its arched back.

"Hello," she whispered to the pottery.

Carefully tipping the rabbit upside down, she searched for initials. What she saw made her suck in her breath in a great gasp.

Jack Graham. Kiln #43. She looked back into the rabbit's eyes and exhaled in awe. "My Lord. You're a piece from the missing kiln."

She cradled the clay rabbit in her hands, cupping its body as if it were a tiny sparrow fallen from the nest.

Suddenly, the silence in the room seemed to lengthen. The twitter of mockingbirds in the yard and the buzzing of honeybees and cicadas faded. Molly held the rabbit against her and felt the life throbbing within the clay. She sensed its journey through the riverbed, saw the spinning wheel slick with water, the potter's hands, and felt the night curl around it as it dried in the summer air. A strong feeling of protectiveness enveloped her. No one would take this piece from her. It had a story to tell and she would listen to its wordless tale.

"Poor thing. Have you been in the dark for a long time? Don't worry, that's all over now. You're coming home with me."

And then, in a house that had seemed completely empty moments ago, a piercing scream shattered the silence.

"Nnnoooooooooo!" echoed a man's voice. The elongated syllables were filled with pain.

Molly sprinted into Bunny's wing, the rabbit clutched tightly in her hand.

At first all she saw was the estate's gardener on his knees, rocking back and forth and sobbing "no" over and over. As Molly reached out to touch him, to comfort him, she saw Bunny.

Bunny was laid out on the sofa as if she had swooned, her yellow blouse torn through the center of her chest where a bullet had bit through the fabric. Blood was splattered in thin droplets all over the white sofa and wall. Dark red liquid had dripped from her back and pooled onto the hardwood floor, forming an oval stain. The gardener was kneeling in it as he held Bunny's limp hand and wailed.

A pink pillow lay at Bunny's feet, its fibrous filling scattered over her legs and the floor. Whoever had killed Bunny had shot her at close range through the pillow. It had been blown apart by the force of the bullet.

Molly blinked, unable to believe what her eyes were telling her. She stared dumbly at the red blood pooled by her shoe. Bunny was dead, right in front of her. She took a step back, shaking herself out of shock.

Her first action was to stop the gardener from screaming. She grabbed his shoulder and shook him.

"What's your name?" she demanded firmly.

The man turned his coffee-colored eyes to her. She almost flinched when she saw the agony reflected in his face. "I am . . . my name is Emmanuel."

"Come away, Emmanuel," she said gently, tugging at his arm to get him to stand up. When he wouldn't budge, she pulled him harder. "We have to call the police. Please. Come with me."

Mindlessly, the grieving man stood and followed her. His loud sobs had turned to weeping, and Molly instinctively put her arm around his waist and propelled him to the kitchen. After calling the police and reporting the murder, she put the kettle on and searched in the cupboards until she found packets of tea.

"I'm sorry," she said a few minutes later as she poured Emmanuel a strong cup of tea. "Drink this, it will help calm you down. Do you think you can you tell me what happened?"

Emmanuel took a deep sip and looked at her as tears ran down his cheeks. "I don't know. I just . . . found her. Someone shot her. I was outside and I didn't hear anything." He shook his head. "I loved her, but they will think I did it. I am the gardener! A foreigner! They will think it was me, that I—"

"No one is going to assume you shot Mrs. Staunton," Molly cut him off before he became hysterical. "Do you own a gun?"

"No," Emmanuel replied tonelessly.

"Well, that's a good start in proving your innocence. Were there any guns in the house?"

"Mr. Staunton owned some old shotguns. All his stuff is gone now though."

"And there won't be any gunshot residue on your hands either. Did you see anyone around the house this morning?" Molly asked. "Any cars come down the driveway?"

Emmanuel tried to concentrate. "I was working by the tennis court most of day. I can't see much from back there and I was using the hedge trimmers. They are very loud. All I know is Bunny was expecting someone to pick up, uh, *el conejo.*"

Molly didn't recognize the Spanish word. "The what?"

"The rabbit." He gestured at the pottery figure standing on the kitchen counter.

"I came to collect it." Molly sighed. "No other cars?"

Emmanuel buried his face in his hands. Molly thought he would begin crying again, but he suddenly looked up at her with dry, bright eyes. "I did see one! I don't know cars, but it was white."

"And big, more like a van instead of a car?"

"Si, yes, higher than a car." He raised his hand up.

At that moment, the police burst into the front hall. An officer strode into the kitchen and asked to be shown the body. Remarkably calm, Molly directed Emmanuel to stay put and led the police to the body. As she explained her presence to the officer in charge, an Officer Bennett, Emmanuel was led in. "I tell you!" he moaned. "I loved her! I did not kill her!"

"Will you need an interpreter?" the second one asked unkindly. Emmanuel ignored him.

Bennett quickly intervened, warning his men to keep their mouths shut before turning curious eyes to Molly. "I thought you were just picking up a piece of pottery. You sound like you might have an idea who the killer is."

Molly thought about the threatening voice mail and shivered. Then she grew angry. How dare someone try to scare her? She would make them sorry. If the caller was the murderer, Molly would help put the villain behind bars.

She returned Bennett's gaze and surprised him by saying, "Not just an idea. I absolutely know who the killer is."

• • •

In what seemed like an hour later, Bennett ordered a junior officer to pick up the person Molly identified as a suspect. He then warned the other cop to meet him back at the station. He told Molly she would have to come to the station as well to fill out a report.

Holding Emmanuel with gentle firmness by the arm, Bennett gave orders to the forensic unit and to the coroner before escorting Molly and Emmanuel to his car.

"Bennett!" an officer called after him. "Let me swab those two for residue."

"Me, too?" Molly asked.

"We have to check for gunpowder. It just rules you out as suspects," Bennett replied and nodded at the officer. "Go ahead, Frank."

Both Molly and Emmanuel's hands were swabbed. Frank shook his head and turned away to help his crew unload equipment.

"No traces on either of you," Bennett explained, holding open the car door.

At the small police station, Molly was given a tepid cup of coffee and some stale cheese crackers while she went through her statement. There were only two interview rooms as most of the building was comprised of offices and holding cells, so Molly and Emmanuel were seated at tables next to each other. Bennett sat across from Molly and asked questions as another officer took notes on a pad.

She calmly explained her reasons for being at the Staunton residence as well as how she knew the identity of the killer. The only thing about the experience that unnerved her was the presence of the tape recorder on the table.

"Just try to ignore it," Bennett suggested, watching Molly stare at the spinning disks inside the recorder.

As she was in the middle of describing the voice mail message she had received, an officer led a petite woman clad in a black pantsuit into the station. When the woman's angry gaze fell upon Molly, she lurched free of the man's grip, grabbed a stapler off the nearest desk, and ran straight for her.

"You fat, nosy bitch! I'll kill you too!" Susan Black screamed.

Bennett leapt up and intercepted Susan's raised hand in a quick, fluid motion. Susan fumed and struggled beneath his iron grasp, her eyes never leaving Molly's face. Her hatred twisted her features into an ugly mask.

"It was *my* money! *Mine!* I deserved it for sleeping with that disgusting bastard! For keeping his stupid secrets! I deserved it *all!* And you, you interfering little *bitch* . . . !" Susan was dragged away, spitting and yelling every obscenity Molly had ever heard until the doors leading to the cells clanked behind her.

Bennett sank back into his chair, took a sip of coffee, and grimaced.

"Absolute swill. Please continue with your statement, Miss Appleby. I plan to let our real suspect calm down a moment before I ask for her side of the story." He smirked. "Though that might take quite a while."

• • •

By dinnertime, Molly was luxuriating in the scalding water of Clara's hot tub with a large mojito near at hand.

Clara hovered nearby, uncharacteristically ruffled by her daughter's depiction of the day's events.

Finally, Molly scolded Clara until she settled into a nearby lounge chair, making room for her favorite cat, a twenty-two-pound apricot-colored tabby named Tiny Purr. Clara began sipping rapidly from a crystal tumbler filled with Crown Royal and water.

"Doesn't look like you've got much water in there, Ma," Molly teased.

"Hah! You're lucky there's even any ice in here. I don't know how you can settle for a tutti-frutti drink at a time like this. Poor Bunny! And my poor baby! You must be fit to be tied!"

"You know sugar makes everything all right for me. I'm tired, but at least this mystery is almost solved," Molly said as she sank deeper into the warm water.

"Oh, there can't be any more surprises left. Susan killed them both. She must have! She was at the kiln opening and she hated both the Stauntons," Clara said with finality.

"We'll see what Officer Bennett comes up with. Now . . . look in that box." Molly pointed to a side table. "That's the piece of pottery I went to pick up."

Molly watched as her mother lifted the rabbit from the box. Her own feelings of discovery were mirrored on her mother's face as her jaw slacked with shock.

"Kiln forty-three! I can't believe it!"

"Isn't he beautiful?" Molly said proudly.

"He is. He's wonderful." Her mother looked at her. "So there *was* a surviving kiln load. But what happened to the rest of the pieces?"

"I don't know. I need to find out more about Jack Graham."

Clara held the rabbit up triumphantly, her worries vanishing like the ice in her drink. "Well, you'll have the chance next weekend."

"How?"

Clara produced a postcard, which she had been using as a bookmark, and smiled widely. "Jack Graham is having his first kiln opening in two years. It's a small, private affair for a select group of friends and collectors."

"How did you get your hands on an invitation?" Molly asked.

"Donald, of course."

"That man is a wonder," Molly said.

The two women sat in silence, admiring the pottery rabbit that basked in the glow of the waning summer sun.

Once her cocktail was finished, Molly dried off and picked up the clay piece, gazing at it with maternal tenderness. Crickets sang and a few fireflies began to burn in the purpling sky.

"Only one question remains. If that kiln wasn't supposed to exist, how did George-Bradley get a hold of you?"

Chapter 15

"**D**o tell, Miss Marple. Was Susan Black really wearing gold lamé shoes when she was arrested? I have a bet with Francis over this fashion detail." Clayton leaned a hip clad in suede jeans on Molly's desk.

She tried to remember. "Yes, I think she was."

"Lord have mercy! Who does she think she is, Faith Hill? Now I owe Francis a dinner at Cafe Luna. Damn. Oops, time to dash." Clayton jumped up and scurried away as Matt came out of his office carrying a huge bouquet of wildflowers.

"These are for you." He smiled and laid them on her desk. "The hero of the hour. Or . . . er . . . heroine of the hour. Feel up to going to lunch?"

"Absolutely. Thank you." Molly's stomach rumbled in anticipation. "Let's go," she laughed.

Later, seated at a cozy table at a small Italian eatery, Molly told Matt all about her visit to Bunny's.

"How did you know the killer was Susan Black?" Matt asked as they buttered slices of warm, crusty bread.

"I saw her car at the auction. A white Mercedes SUV. I wondered where she had gotten the money for that car, the pottery, and her clothes. She has no regular job that I know of. I guess George-Bradley had treated her quite well when they were together and she didn't want to stop living the good life."

"But didn't you say they'd been broken up for a while?" Matt asked, twirling spaghetti in meat sauce around on his fork.

"Yeah, but there was that thing Bunny whispered in Susan's ear about the car ride in the backwoods. I guess I'll never know everything Bunny said or what was in that letter, but it was enough to get her killed."

"And seeing her . . . body didn't bother you?"

Molly cut one of her herbed meatballs in two and sent sauce flying onto the white tablecloth. "Oh, dear." She colored. "Sorry, I've never been good at eating Italian without getting sauce somewhere it doesn't belong. Did seeing Bunny bother me? No, it didn't. She didn't seem like a real person anymore, you know? She was more like a wax figure from Madame Tussauds."

"That's the way it was in med school too. I was pretty nervous about my first anatomy class, but it wasn't that bad. The cadavers weren't like real people anymore. They were more like CPR dummies. At least it helped to think of them that way. If I'd thought of someone as having once been a parent or a brother or sister, I wouldn't have learned a thing."

Molly studied him. "Can I ask you why you didn't finish?"

Matt peered at her defensively, and then his face instantly softened. "Sure you can. It's just painful to talk about. In the summer before my last year, my parents were killed in a car accident." He paused and took a deep drink of Chianti. "I had to take care of all the arrangements—it was just my younger brother and me—and by the time the estate was straightened out, school had started and I wasn't ready to go back. I felt too broken to go back."

"Of course you did. I'm so sorry, Matt." Molly covered his hand with hers.

"I might enroll again someday. I still want to be a doctor," Matt said as he squeezed her hand in return, "but I can't see leaving work now. Not when I have such good company right across the hall."

• • •

"Are you going to quit?" Swanson barked at Molly after she returned to her desk following her lunch with Matt.

"Why?" she asked, horrified that her piece on Sam Chance might have been poorly written.

"Because you seem more involved with hard-boiled crime stories these days than reporting on antiques and collectibles. I want a piece that finishes this pottery series off with a bang."

Molly squirmed as Swanson's foul breath hit her in the face. "I *have* found one more potter I'd like to interview."

"And perhaps you'd like to tell me about this mystery man."

"His name is Jack Graham. He's another Seagrove potter, but Sam Chance said he doesn't do interviews anymore."

"Any reason?" Swanson's curiosity was aroused.

Molly repeated Sam's words and how he'd grown uncomfortable and had refused to give out any information about Graham aside from warning her to stay away. Swanson's eyes lit up at the thought of a dramatic secret adding more spice to the paper. The recent edition, replete with details on George-Bradley's death and Hillary Keane's arrest, had created record highs in circulation.

"You get that interview with Graham. I don't care how you get it, just see that you do." Swanson broke off to cough up something liquid into his yellowed handkerchief.

"I'm on it," Molly said, backing away from the desk in disgust. "I'll try to get something lined up with him this weekend."

But before the weekend's kiln opening, she needed to discover more about this potter whose only surviving piece from an entire kiln had been a small, unglazed rabbit.

• • •

The next day, Molly headed for the library at Duke University, an old, gray stone building with Tudor-style windows and a sprawling layout of endless rooms. Filled with students poring over books or conducting group study sessions in low whispers, the atmosphere was both quiet and lively.

As posters of Lincoln, Harriet Tubman, and the Wright Brothers cast knowing but affable glances down upon her, she began searching through databases for newspaper articles on Jack Graham.

Scanning through the summary lines on the computer screen, Molly noted that most of these were articles about the uniqueness of Graham's work or short pieces detailing his kiln openings. His name popped up in several other searches relating to the Seagrove area and its potters, but nothing appeared about his personal life.

Molly read everything available to her, printing out a few of the articles reviewing Graham's work in order to improve her own knowledge of the talented craftsman. Nothing indicated that Graham had faced any "trouble," but then again, none of the articles mentioned anything personal about Graham except for his age and the family's history of pottery making. Stumped, Molly approached the reference desk to seek help.

A tall, pale-faced male librarian with a white button-down shirt and frayed brown pants greeted her kindly. His round, thick glasses enlarged his greenish eyes and amplified his hooked nose, giving the impression of a friendly turtle. There was nothing slow about his fingers, however, and when Molly explained what she was looking for, his hands flew like startled finches over the keys.

"Jack Graham," he said, lips crinkling in concentration, "a Seagrove potter, if I'm not mistaken."

"Yes."

"Known for his perfect form and the brilliant hues of his glazes," he continued.

"That's right." Molly was impressed.

"The Archives Database will provide birth information, so you'll know his age and place of birth, but that's not much." His fingers continued to peck at the keyboard. "Let's see what the local press has to say."

Results danced over the screen in black and blue lines of text. The librarian did not seem pleased. He sighed heavily, stroking the gray stubble peppering his chin.

"Once again, progress is halted due to lack of funding."

"What happened?" Molly asked, disappointed. Mr. Turtle seemed as capable as a magician waving his wand over a black hat. She had expected those nimble fingers to pull out the white rabbit of news articles on the life of Jack Graham.

"The microfiche of the Asheboro papers, which would have covered all events occurring in Seagrove, have not been downloaded into the database yet. Their branch needs to link with our database, but they only have one or two computers. The state has made huge cuts from library budgets everywhere. The smaller libraries are really suffering." He shrugged. "Remember this during the next election year."

"So if they can't afford to have the database, are all the area newspaper articles on microfiche?"

"Probably, yes. I'm afraid you'll have to go to the main branch in Asheboro and look at films the old-fashioned way."

Molly thanked Mr. Turtle for his help, returned to her car, and headed for the interstate. She'd have a quick lunch before driving an hour and a half to Asheboro once again. She pulled off I-85 at a cafeteria and selected an array of homemade foods for lunch, including macaroni and cheese, black-eyed peas, and bread pudding with vanilla custard sauce for dessert.

The librarian at the local branch was an older woman with curly, paper-white hair. It was so thin that her pink scalp winked out in places like bare patches on the lawn. Her eyes were sharp blue and sparkled with vivacity. She patted Molly on the hand after listening to her request and handed her several old index boxes.

"These are the newspaper films we've got on file. You just figure out what issue you want and bring the card up here. I'll get the films and set you up on the reader."

"Thank you." Molly made herself comfortable in an oversized pink chair by the window and began flipping through the cards. Each card contained a summary of the important articles of the week, sorted by subject. She began flipping through the "Arts" sections, musing over the differences between Duke's database and this library's boxes of yellow aged index cards.

As the afternoon wore on, Molly found several references to Jack Graham's work. She had a small stack of cards laid aside with short articles covering his kiln openings. As the librarian leaned over her to line up the rolls of microfiche, Molly caught a sweet, familiar whiff of vanilla. Molly always burned vanilla candles in her house, and her favorite coffee flavor was French vanilla.

"Anything wrong, dear?" the librarian's mellifluous voice inquired.

"Not at all," she assured the librarian. "By the way, you smell lovely."

The librarian beamed and walked off, leaving Molly to scroll through pages of film, printing out any articles where Jack Graham's name appeared. She then collected her pile of printouts and returned to her soft chair to read, hoping at least to learn which buyers were present at each sale. Would any of these short pieces hold clues about Graham's personal life?

Most of the articles were about Graham's pieces being exhibited in the area's museums or about his biannual kiln openings. Molly began by numbering the articles on the openings, so she could discover in which month kiln number forty-three had *not* been produced. She paused over any photographs from the sales, noting familiar figures such as George-Bradley, Hillary Keane, Clara's friend Donald, and even Clara herself. Most of these were taken before the kiln opening began, when frenzied buyers stood with their hands resting on the pieces of their choice, carefully guarding them until the time they could check out.

By kiln number twenty-five, Molly noticed that Jack Graham had switched to the lottery system. Now photos showed buyers drawing from a hat and studying their numbers with glee or dismay. Those with low numbers picked first, snatching the most singular pieces from the sale. By the end of the lottery, only a few plain vases or ordinary bowls remained. They were all beautiful, but not as unique as the one peacock-incised floor vase or elaborate salt-glazed candelabra that the lucky holders of low lottery numbers had seized in the first few rounds of drawings.

In fact, one photo illustrated a woman throwing her hands in the air in disgust as she discovered what number she had drawn. Molly smiled at the photo, as it was so typical of the emotions displayed all over in the world of collecting. She examined the article further, admiring a photograph of neat rows of pottery in Graham's yard, the words of praise from the local museum curators, and the attendance his work drew for county festivals. So far, Graham's life seemed trouble-free.

As she continued to number the articles, the late afternoon sun began to grow weary and rested its heavy head among the pines dotting the horizon. The librarian hummed at her desk, her small hands flipping through the pages of a colorful children's book. Molly watched her, wondering if she would know anything more about Graham. After all, she had probably lived in the area for a long time, and if there were any noteworthy personal information about him, surely a local person would know all about it.

"Ma'am?" she interrupted the librarian's reading.

"How can I help you, dear?"

"I seem to keep striking out and I don't want to go home empty-handed," Molly said truthfully.

"Those films didn't help?" The bright eyes were sympathetic.

"No. I'm looking for information on Jack Graham, the potter. Do you know him?"

The woman's wrinkled forehead gathered into itself as she thought. "I've heard of him, yes. He makes pottery, but not much these days I hear."

Molly showed her the numbered stack of articles. "About two years ago, in the spring, he should have had kiln opening number forty-three, but he didn't. I'm trying to figure out why."

"Well, let me see." The librarian shuffled back over to the drawers holding the microfiche. "We'll have to look at that year's events some more. Maybe there was a fire or something . . . a particular hardship or catastrophe that prevented him from working."

Molly digested the librarian's comment and then seized upon an idea. "Fire, maybe . . . or snow!" she suggested, excitedly. "Isn't that the winter we had those two big storms back to back and no one had power for weeks?"

"It is, it is." The blue eyes sparkled.

"And he might not have been able to work without power," Molly continued.

The librarian loaded in the film, and the two women sat side by side and read about the aftermath of the two blizzards. North Carolina rarely saw snow, and when it came, it was usually a light dusting that sent people dashing out to the store for bread, milk, and eggs. Driving conditions were treacherous because the state had no equipment for snow removal. Still, people who could barely drive well in rain went racing off in a state of panic to the grocery, causing dozens of accidents each time a cluster of snowflakes flew.

But these blizzards were different. They each piled six to eight inches of snow in some places, downing power lines and covering the roads completely. After the two storms had dumped their loads of heavy powder, a rain had fallen, covering the world in a clear layer of sparkling, menacing ice.

Molly remembered using her gas logs to stay warm and sleeping on the sofa for a week. With no electricity, she had to reread all of Jane Austen's novels and put together puzzles by candlelight, thrilled at having a week off school and enjoying the adventure of donning snow gear to walk a mile to the grocery store, where she waited for two hours in line to buy cat food and granola bars.

However, she lived in a populated development, and by the second week her power was restored. And even when her car had been snowed in, she could walk fairly easily to the store and was able to use her cell phone to call her friends and family. Others had not been so lucky.

Out in the country, many people had no source of energy except for small wood-burning stoves. They had no access to grocery stores and had to rely on whatever canned goods were at hand. Dozens of fatalities occurred from car accidents. Worse than that, several people had died from hypothermia when they got trapped in thigh-high snow heading to town on the remote back roads. When the snow melted, their bodies were discovered near the road or curled inside their cars, where they had gotten stuck too far from town and too far from home.

"Maybe that's it." Molly turned to her helper, thinking about the news stories she'd seen on TV about the serious conditions people in the country faced during those two weeks. "What about that storm could have changed Jack Graham's life? A friend of mine told me that the family had had some trouble. Did they . . . did he lose someone in that storm?"

The librarian didn't answer. She seemed lost in thought.

"Ma'am?"

"Oh," the woman said and flashed her a smile. "I was just trying to remember. And call me Harriet, dear. There's something scratching at my brain but I can't figure out what it is. We can check the obituaries for the months before Graham was supposed to have his opening. He had one in the spring and one in the fall, correct?" Molly nodded. "But we've got to shake a tail feather because it's almost closing time," the librarian added.

Molly looked at her watch in alarm. She only had twenty minutes left. If she didn't find something today, she'd have to make the hour-and-a-half trip again after the auction this weekend.

"Don't fret." Harriet held out two rolls of fresh film. "You check the months you have and I'll look back in the October and November obituaries."

"Thank you, that's very kind."

The two women fell silent, scanning the names of those who had died between October and April, looking for a familiar name or face to jump out from where it was buried in positives and negatives within the screen. Graham's openings were regularly held in September and April, early in the morning on vibrant, crisp days. Molly was loading in the film for February when Harriet gasped beside her.

"What is it?" Molly asked.

"I'm remembering." The blue eyes shifted slowly from the screen to the sinking sun out the window. "There was something about one of his children."

"I read in a biographical piece that he had two."

"Something terrible," Harriet said mournfully as she turned back to her machine and began hastily loading in the October film. "There was something about his little girl."

Molly abandoned her machine and slid her chair closer to Harriet's, comforted by her vanilla scent and the fruity perfumes of her hair.

In the silent room, Molly felt a strong foreboding grip her. They were about to uncover something horrible, something that shouldn't be rifled through by a complete stranger.

Molly found she no longer wanted to know what happened to disturb the balance of this man's life. He was a gifted potter, a husband, and a father. What was she doing here, searching for his secrets? It was his life; his reasons for taking a season off of pottery making were his own. She was no tabloid journalist.

Shaken, she reached out to tell Harriet to stop, that it didn't matter, that there were others to interview, that she had been wrong to come. Her hand reached out, touched the soft fabric of Harriet's cotton blouse, and rested there.

"Here!" Harriet breathed, arresting the words on Molly's lips.

She pointed to an obituary toward the middle of the first column. Hesitating, Molly looked at the photograph of a smiling little girl with long pigtail braids tied with gingham bows. She was missing one of her front teeth and large dimples dented her shiny cheeks. She wore overalls over a T-shirt and looked impatient to be on the move again, yet too good-natured not to smile sweetly for what must have been a school picture. Molly read:

Graham
Lilly Ann Graham, age 9, departed this life

Saturday, October 3rd, to join the Lord. She is survived by her loving parents, Jack and Leslie Graham, and by her brother, Jack Junior, age 7. Lilly Ann was in the third grade at Seagrove Elementary School, where she excelled in art and science classes. She played competitive soccer and recently starred in her class play, "Many Moons." Lilly Ann will be remembered for her loving, generous spirit. Memorial services will be held Monday, October 5th, from noon until one p.m. at the Piney Hollow Methodist Church, 1500 North Bramble Drive. Interment will be at the Seagrove Memorial Cemetery. In lieu of flowers, the family suggests contributions to be made to the Girl Scouts of America, of which Lilly Ann was an enthusiastic member.

Molly sat back in her chair, her hand covering her mouth. What had happened to Graham's little girl?

"How horrible," she muttered, blinking back tears as she stared at Lilly Ann's face. "That poor family."

Harriet turned to her, blue eyes liquid as they reflected the light from the screen. "Now I remember," she whispered, then turned back to the machine and went back to the front page of the same edition. "Look."

Molly felt a shiver ripple up her arms. One of the bold headlines read, *Seagrove Girl Killed By Hit-and-Run.*

"They found her in the road," Harriet began, speaking so softly that Molly could barely hear her. "She was already dead. She had been riding her bike . . . I remember that. Here's a picture of it, see?" Molly unwillingly leaned forward to see the crushed and twisted metal remains. Harriet continued, "I remember her mother telling a reporter that she never let Lilly Ann go too far from home. She had some kind of medical condition. She was allowed to ride down to the creek in one direction and to the neighbor's in the other. That day, she was going to the creek to sail some paper boats she'd made at school. They were still in her backpack."

"How unbelievably awful," Molly said with deep sorrow.

"They never caught the driver. He hit her and drove off. There were no witnesses. Back where most of those potters live, there aren't too many other folks around."

Harriet sighed, turning away from the tragic headline. "That was the worst of it . . . that whoever killed this sweet little girl probably never stopped, never even pulled over to see if she was alive."

"And no one was ever arrested?" Molly asked in disbelief.

"No one." Harriet closed her eyes for a moment. "He got away. But his time will come. That's the way things work in this world."

Molly was stunned. As Harriet pressed the "print" button and noiselessly moved off to begin her closing tasks, Molly remained immobile in her wooden chair. Finally, as the humming of the machines clicked off to silence, Molly let her head sink into her hands, her eyes straying to the window.

At last, all of the pieces of the puzzle about George-Bradley's death fell together. Molly now knew who his killer was and the murderer was not Susan Black. What should have been a triumphant moment filled her with a heavy weariness. And she would still need to prove herself right before mentioning what she knew to anyone else.

The surrendering sun had disappeared behind the blue-black line of trees and long snakelike shadows crept like tendrils across the library floor. The other people who had been quietly reading or typing at computers had departed. The fluorescent lights fizzled and strained to make up for the departure of natural light. Molly turned full circle before her stack of paper and notecards, searching for a sign of life.

But she was alone with no comfort left in the dying day.

Chapter 16

Potters have always catered to children—in part, because children have always been drawn to their shops to witness the magical growth of a jug on the wheel or to take part in the excitement of kiln burning.
—Charles G. Zug III, form *Turners and Burners*

Jack Graham's kiln opening for kiln number fifty took place under a rented tent in his backyard at the reasonable hour of ten o'clock on a fine, late summer morning. Two picnic tables held the seventy-five extraordinary pieces of pottery to be sold before lunch.

Riding to Seagrove with Clara and Donald, Molly kept opening the shoebox on her lap to gaze sadly upon the face of her little rabbit. She planned to return him to the Grahams, the rightful owners, and hopefully put an end to all the mysteries that had begun just a few weeks ago at another kiln opening.

"So tell Donald why Susan Black killed Bunny. He hasn't heard the whole story," Clara prompted from the front seat.

Molly took a sip of creamy hazelnut coffee. "One of my co-workers, Clayton, worms the best tidbits from a friend of his from the *Times*. This reporter interviewed Susan right after her arrest. Apparently, Susan knew all about the bearer bonds George-Bradley had stashed away and was waiting for the right time to steal them from the Stauntons' house. Her plan was to grab the certificates and leave the state. That's why she never called me back to schedule an interview."

"I take it Bunny didn't oblige her," Donald stated.

"I guess not. Susan claimed that George-Bradley had been saving that money so that once he and Bunny were divorced, he could start a new life with her. He told Susan about his hiding place in the wall but Susan hadn't counted on Bunny being home. That was Bunny's regular day to play bridge at her sister's house, but she had changed her schedule in order to meet Lex's employee. Of course, it was me who came to collect the rabbit and not someone from the auction gallery."

"But Susan showed up at the Stauntons' carrying a gun!" Clara exclaimed.

"Yes, and when the police picked her up she was loading a box of pottery into her car. She had fake identification papers and was planning to live a quiet life of ease in the Caymans. She also showed no signs of remorse. She felt she was owed those bonds, and she was going to get them no matter what."

Donald shook his head. "But they broke up two years ago, so why did she decide to go after this money now?"

Molly shrugged. "I guess she figured with George-Bradley dead, she could take the bonds and no one would be the wiser. Susan knew where the bearer bonds were hidden and she must have assumed that Bunny knew nothing about the secret panel. So she took a chance and went to get them without thinking about the consequences of getting caught. However, Susan did not seem like a stable person in the police station. I mean, who attacks an enemy with a stapler?"

"I'm glad you can be so flippant about that," Clara complained. "As for your poor mother . . . the images I have from your recent events! How can you get yourself in the middle of such a mess? If you were at home with a few children to keep you busy—"

"Anyway," Molly interrupted as Donald winked at her in the rearview mirror. "It looks like Bunny's estate, which is worth over three million dollars, will be divided between her sister and Emmanuel." She paused and smiled, thinking of Emmanuel's kind, weathered face. "When I last talked to Officer Bennett, he told me that Susan confessed to killing Bunny but refused to admit that she left me a threatening voice mail message."

"Ah, well." Clara's tone was dismissive. "You said yourself she wasn't stable. Look at all that rage she kept inside."

"Well, that's that," Donald pronounced. "Now, what about our friend Hillary? Any news on that front?"

"Actually, Clayton told me that Mr. Keane is facing a long jail sentence. Apparently he has been stealing pottery from both potters and collectors for years and selling it to buyers up north. He was dashing off to a rendezvous in Hendersonville to sell a huge inventory of stolen pieces when he almost hit that jogger."

"What?" Clara shrieked. "I thought he was only taking pieces from George-Bradley every now and then."

"No, he has been stealing pottery for years. He even lifted pieces from three area museums during special exhibits. The FBI's Antiquity Recovery Division is very pleased to have him in jail. Keane still had the museum pieces in his garage, and now they are proudly back on display in their rightful homes."

"But that still doesn't explain his motives," Clara said.

"Pure greed, Ma. You know how it is in the world of collecting. Keane wanted the big house, the period furniture, and a prime pottery collection, but his salary working as a small-town pharmacist couldn't finance his dreams. In fact, he has a famous nickname on the Internet."

"What was that?" Donald asked expectantly.

"The Pirate of Pottery," Molly said.

"I just can't believe it," Clara muttered. "You think you know someone. He seemed the very portrait of a gentleman on the outside. All that time envy was burning a hole in him on the inside. Who would have thought?"

Molly looked down at the rabbit. "Some people are really good at hiding their true feelings."

• • •

Jack Graham was stocky, muscular, and completely bald. One weathered hand rhythmically stroked his short brown beard as he waited for everyone to take his or her seats. Molly noticed that there were more people present than there were pieces of pottery. Folks had come to welcome the Grahams back to their former lifestyle—one that included public kiln openings. It had been over two years since they had had an open sale. Molly recognized several local potters as well as a member of the local press.

"Thank y'all for comin'." Jack hushed the crowd with a soft commanding voice. "Just so there's no question of cheatin', Jack Junior is gonna pass the 'Numbers Hat' today. When you hear your number called, go on up and pick your piece. We've got some folks to help you wrap it when you're ready to go. Please help yourself to some fried chicken and biscuits too. Leslie's been cooking all morning."

The crowd applauded as Jack's wife, Leslie, blushed at the attention. Molly recognized her from C.C.'s kiln opening. She had helped Eileen serve the sweet tea and cookies.

With a clear view of Mrs. Graham, Molly could now see that Leslie was well into her second trimester of pregnancy. Her long, auburn hair was shiny with good health and her freckled face glowed with anticipation. How happy she must be to see her husband back at work and to be expecting another child.

Molly knew that no parent ever finishes grieving over a lost child, and both the Grahams had trace amounts of sadness in their eyes. Their sorrow was buried in the lines at the corners of their mouths. Nine-year-old dimpled Jack Junior, on the other hand, bounded around the buyers, letting them draw numbered tickets from a battered top hat.

"I forgot to mention," Donald said, clearing his throat and sliding a postcard into Molly's hand as Jack Junior headed their way. "My friend Blake can't make the sale so you can use his card to get a number. It wouldn't do for you to go home empty-handed."

Molly's eyes grew round in wonder and she planted a kiss on Donald's cheek. "Thank you, Donald!"

Clara beamed at her friend. "You are a prince among frogs," she said as she patted Donald on the arm.

Jack Junior reached Clara first and she put her hand in his deep hat and took a ticket. Donald drew next. Then, it was Molly's turn to pick.

"Donald!" Clara quickly exclaimed. "How did you get so lucky?"

Donald slyly showed Molly his ticket. He had drawn the number three. He would be the third person to select a piece of pottery. His eyes gleamed in excitement and relief. Clara had drawn number thirty-two, and Molly had drawn number fifty. She certainly wasn't disappointed, as she hadn't expected to own a piece at all.

Excitement began to build as the numbers were handed out. Unlike at C.C.'s opening, there was no hostility between the buyers. No one had to race to seize the piece they wanted. This selection was all left to chance, so there was no one to get angry with except for Lady Luck. Everyone seemed pleased to simply be in the audience to witness Jack Graham's return to the public eye.

As Donald's number was called, he carefully walked up to a pair of tall candlesticks glazed in red brown, each encircled by a green and black striped snake. Later, Molly watched with baited breath as her mother chose a large white and brown swirled serving bowl. Clara reminded Molly that the swirls came from using two types of clay and that it was extremely difficult to create even spirals when mixing clays. Jack Graham's swirls had turned out perfectly.

Molly handed her number to her mother.

"Will you pick a piece for me?" she asked quietly, her mind on other matters.

"Of course, but why?" Clara asked, surprised.

"I want a word with Leslie while people are paying attention to the selection process," Molly explained and then excused herself.

She made her way to the back porch of the Grahams' house, where Leslie sat watching the next buyer deliberate over two of her husband's pieces. Molly introduced herself, and as Leslie stood to shake her hand, Jack Junior interrupted and begged for a soda before lunch.

"Not now, Jack. Those drinks are for the guests. You can have some juice or milk from in the house."

Sulking, Jack flopped down from the porch and went to hang over the food table.

"You'd think I never fed that boy." Leslie smiled indulgently as she watched her son. She turned to Molly. "I've read your pieces in *Collector's Weekly*. I think you've done some good for the potters around here. I believe Sam Chance has gotten some extra business."

"I sure hope so," Molly replied, flattered. Leslie was one of those rare individuals with an easy, sincere manner that made her attractive to members of both genders. Molly liked her immediately. Perhaps it was her sprinkling of freckles or her lively green eyes, but Molly felt completely at ease with Leslie Graham. "Do you think I could get an interview with your husband sometime this week?"

Leslie paused. "I don't see why not. We could use the publicity now that he's back in business. Oh!" she exclaimed, putting a hand on her belly.

"Are you all right?"

"I sure am. It was just a kick and a hard one too! Come on into the kitchen and we'll check the calendar. With all Jack Junior's baseball and soccer games, we have to plan our lives around him."

"How far along are you?" Molly asked as they went inside the shotgun-style house.

"Twenty-four weeks and counting," Leslie said, rubbing her lower back.

"Do you know what you're having?"

"Yes, another boy." Leslie smiled at Molly. "Another soccer player too, I'd say. I hardly slept a wink last night. Please sit down."

Molly laughed. Then she remembered the shoebox she was carrying. "I have something that I believe rightfully belongs to you."

Leslie looked up from the calendar she was holding and eyed the shoebox warily. "To me?"

"Well, to your family . . ." Molly faltered. She unwrapped the rabbit so that it could explain itself.

Leslie's face turned pale. A hand fluttered up to her chest. She seemed on the point of flight but changed her mind and, with a deep breath, sank down in a chair next to Molly.

She touched the rabbit's face as tears sprang into her eyes.

"This was meant to be a gift for my daughter," she whispered, looking down at the piece. "She was killed by a hit-and-run about the same time as Jack was firing this kiln load. After Lilly Ann's death, he smashed every piece. He was so angry that the driver was never caught. We both were. We didn't know what to do with that anger."

Leslie dabbed her eyes with a dishcloth. Molly looked down at the table, not knowing how to console her hostess. "I didn't mean to upset you. I thought you might want it back. I'm very sorry."

Molly was sure Leslie would ask how she'd come by the rabbit but the potter's wife gazed out the window. As her eyes scanned the yard, the number of people clustering around the food table drew her attention.

"Oh, dear." She sniffed and covered up the rabbit with the box lid. "They're eating already. I'd better go see if everything is set out on the table. Do you mind waiting here for a moment?"

"Of course not," Molly answered, feeling terrible.

After Leslie left, Jack Junior entered the kitchen and offered Molly a friendly hello.

"Where's Ma?" he asked, looking around the room.

"She went outside to check the food."

"Oh, good, then I can have a soda," he pronounced, giving himself permission. He opened up the fridge and brought a liter bottle over to Molly.

"Can you get the top off?" he asked her.

Molly opened the bottle and poured some soda into a small paper cup on the counter. "Don't tell on me," she warned him with a small smile. He promised and then dashed off before his mother returned.

Replacing the cap, Molly returned the bottle to the fridge. A colorful lunchbox caught her eye. Stuffed way back on the bottom shelf, it was one of the metal types, not one of the insulated plastic marvels, mass-produced to generate more money for the latest boy bands or teen queen sensation. This was a Miss Piggy lunchbox, the winsome character from a kid's television show that Molly had always loved.

Without thinking, she reached back behind the loaf of bread and pulled it out. As she opened the latch she realized too late that she was holding the box upside down. Little glass jars with a clear liquid inside rolled out onto the kitchen floor.

Molly quickly scooped up the jars and began arranging them inside the lunchbox. The label on the back of one caught her eye. It was a prescription in Lilly Ann's name. The jars were filled with insulin.

Sitting back on her heels, Molly's mind whirled. She'd been right about the killer's identity but the knowledge was depressing. She was so caught up in the awful truth that she didn't hear Leslie approach until she was just outside the door, scolding Jack Junior in low tones, her voice muffled by the background noise of the crowd. Molly recognized the voice and goose bumps sprouted across the skin of her arms.

"Sorry to keep you wait—" Leslie froze as she saw Molly holding her daughter's lunchbox. She took it from Molly's hands as if it were a wounded bird and slowly, gently closed the lid. The two women locked eyes and it was clear that Leslie realized that her guest had guessed the truth.

"I've cleaned out all the rest of her things," Leslie began. "But not this old lunchbox. It's been sitting in there for two years now. Jack has asked me so many times to take it away, but I just couldn't."

Silently, Molly passed her the last jar of insulin from the floor. Leslie stared at it sorrowfully. "We used to get automatic shipments from a prescription service in Canada. Of course we canceled the service after the accident, but a few weeks ago another one came. Must have been some computer glitch. I viewed it as a sign. I thought I was done being angry"—she wiped away the tears the had begun to trickle down her freckled cheeks—"but when I saw that bastard again at C.C.'s I knew that I hadn't forgiven and could never forget. I didn't mean to kill him, I swear. I just wanted to make him sick, to make him as miserable as I have been without my little girl."

"So you knew George-Bradley was a diabetic?" Molly asked softy.

"Yes. He used to come over here frequently, sniffing around for special deals from Jack and trying to flirt with me. I had always disliked the man, but then, all of a sudden, he stopped coming. He knew that I knew he had killed our daughter."

"He was the driver?" Molly asked gently.

Leslie sagged. "No hard proof, of course. He came over with Bunny a few days after the funeral and he was acting real funny. Wouldn't look either of us in the eye and then stole off into the woods, looking over his shoulder the whole time. I followed him." She took a deep breath. "I had a pair of Lilly Ann's binoculars—she loved to spot deer or rabbits—and saw him at the accident site. He was looking for something by the road that I had already found."

"What was it?"

"A handkerchief. One of those fancy ones with his initials on it. I took it to the police, but they said it proved nothing. His car was clean and he owns some land down this way, so it didn't count as evidence."

Molly remembered how George-Bradley had dabbed his sweaty brow with just such a handkerchief at C.C.'s kiln opening.

Leslie gripped the lunchbox until her knuckles turned white. "I think he was in someone else's car because there wasn't a scratch on his, but I know he hit her. There was a big rain that same afternoon. All the tire tracks were erased. There was no evidence anywhere. But I know the fact that he dropped that handkerchief means that he got out of the car. He got out of the car and saw what he did to my baby and drove away again."

Leslie balled her hands into fists and then placed them on her stomach as she released a deep exhalation.

She turned to Molly, her eyes wide and glassy. "Do you know how many times I have pictured that scene in my head? Do you know how many times I have wondered if she was still alive at the moment? Did that awful man hear her last words? Was she scared? Was she in pain?" She paused again, trying to gather strength, but her shoulders began to shake. Her lips trembled. "And when that devil didn't find the handkerchief, he made his way back to Jack's workshop. God knows why, but he stole the only thing that survived from that kiln. He stole my Lilly Ann's last gift from her daddy. Jack was going to glaze that rabbit bright pink. Her favorite color."

Molly reached out and pulled the weeping woman into her arms. Together, they cried on the kitchen floor until Leslie finally drew away. Miraculously, the party continued outside and no one entered the house. Minutes passed as Leslie composed herself and Molly stared at the floor. Finally, Leslie touched Molly's hand and the women faced each other again. Both of their faces were splotched and puffy from crying.

"Thank you for hearing me out. I am so sorry for leaving you that mean message on your answering machine. Sam Chance told me about your visit and I got scared." She squeezed Molly's hand. "Now I feel like I threatened a friend."

Then she stood, picked up the lunchbox, and resolutely put it in the trash can. As she smoothed down her flowery sundress she said, "We're trying to start our lives over again. My little girl is gone. The man who killed her is gone. Jack is working again. And we have a new Graham on the way. What kind of life this family will live is up to you now."

The scene of the accident became visible in Molly's mind. Lilly Ann racing out of the woods on her bicycle. George-Bradley was with Susan, in her car. He might have been groping her as he drove. Then, the impact. Getting out to see if he had hit a deer. The crumpled bike. The unmoving child.

The horrible secret they'd shared had eventually divided George-Bradley and Susan, but she'd demanded hush money after their breakup. She bought a new Mercedes and expensive pottery with his money, all the while threatening to tell if he should cut her off. Accustomed to her new lifestyle, Susan still wanted her expenses paid for after his death. And she hadn't gone to Bunny's house just for the money. She had also gone to retrieve the incriminating letter.

George-Bradley must have confessed his hit-and-run crime in a sealed letter to his wife, to be read only in the event of his death. After torturing her for years with his lies and his lovers, George-Bradley gave his wife one last nasty dig. He made Bunny aware of his terrible crime, and had boldly confessed who had been in the car with him.

That was the piece of information Bunny had whispered in Susan's ear the day of the auction. Foolish Bunny! She'd boasted that she knew all about the accident, leaving Susan no choice but to come after her for the letter.

George-Bradley had killed Lilly Ann. Now he was dead. Susan had killed Bunny and had also been an accessory to her lover's heinous crime. She was going to spend the rest of her life in jail. The Grahams, who had been through so much pain, were starting to feel the sunlight on their faces again. Work. A new baby. A family made whole.

"I'd better get back to my mother," Molly said, smiling shyly. She looked once more at Leslie's stomach, swollen with new life. With hope. "She'll be saving some of your delicious fried chicken for me."

Gratefully, Leslie took Molly's hands and placed the shoebox in them. "This little guy belongs to you now. He's had some bad treatment and could use some love."

"Thank you. Good luck with everything, Leslie."

The older woman gave her a weak smile. "Please come back and see us. Anytime."

• • •

"She let you keep the rabbit?" Clara asked on the ride home, eyeing the shoebox on her daughter's lap.

"Yes." Molly gazed out the window. It was hard for her to carry on a conversation when her mind was spinning. Leslie had confessed, but nothing was simple about this crime. What should she, a newspaper reporter, do with the truth? All this time she had played detective, and now that she had discovered the answers to all the riddles, she wished she were still in the dark.

After a pause, Molly explained why she had the clay animal. "Leslie said the rabbit brings up bad memories for their family." And she shared the detail about Jack breaking the pieces of kiln number forty-three after Lilly Ann's death. That was the only confidence she shared.

"I can understand that," Clara said. "And I am so glad they are back in the swing of things. Jack's work is better than ever—I hope you got enough pictures—and I hear he is going to have another son. How wonderful! Someone to learn the family business. Jack Junior can't seem to settle down long enough to make a pinch pot. I have never seen such a whirlwind of energy. Have you? Molly?"

After such an emotional day, the vibrations of the car and her mother's prattling proved to be too much. Molly was fast asleep, the shoebox cradled in her arms.

Chapter 17

I have seen many people who have come to understand more about themselves through making things with clay and fire.

—Henry Memmott, from *Discovering Pottery*

Carl Swanson approached Molly's desk chewing feverishly on a piece of gum. He tossed an envelope at her and cleared his throat. "I've got a great assignment lined up for you. You know that TV show, *Hidden Treasures?*" he asked without expecting a reply. "They've agreed to let you spend a week with them this September while they tape an episode in Richmond."

"That does sound like good material for a piece," she agreed and watched as her boss puffed out his chest.

"'Course it does," he snarled in between chews.

Picking up the envelope she asked, "What's this?"

"Look for yourself," he mumbled. "Mr. Macintosh wanted to give you a bonus for helping circulation reach an all-time high."

"Oh, thank you!" Molly was delighted. Mr. Macintosh was the paper's owner.

"Don't thank me," Swanson said truculently. "If I had my way, you wouldn't get paid extra just for doing your job."

As he turned to plod back to his office, Molly noticed a patch on his right arm. Good thing she was getting out of town to cover several auctions this summer since her boss was going to quit smoking. If people thought he was an S.O.B. before . . .

She tore open the envelope and was elated to see the equivalent of a month's pay. Macintosh had been very generous. Molly paused for a moment, feeling the weight of her decision about Leslie's secret cloud her happiness.

Molly had written a short letter to Officer Bennett, explaining that Leslie had given George-Bradley a shot of insulin at C.C.'s kiln opening with the intent of making him ill. Molly also described how George-Bradley had killed Lilly Ann and asked Bennett to look for George-Bradley's confessional letter to Bunny. It was probably somewhere in Susan's house, unless she had had enough time before her arrest to destroy it. Lastly, Molly pleaded with Bennett to go easy on the Grahams, emphasizing Leslie's pregnancy.

It was with shaking hands that Molly had dropped the letter in the mailbox. The truth was a heavy burden, and she did not want to be the one to decide what decisions were to be made in the name of justice.

Afterward, Molly couldn't possibly interview Jack Graham for her final pottery article, but instead wrote a short piece on his return to the public eye and included several descriptive photos from the kiln opening.

Once the article went to print, Molly put all thoughts of secrets and murder out of her head. Every time she glanced at Jack Graham's rabbit, she assured herself that she had done the right thing and tried to focus on what to do with her extra money. Sitting at her desk at the end of the day, an idea bloomed in her mind. She shut down her computer and picked up her purse.

At that moment, the door to Matt's office opened and a familiar pair of long legs attached to a slim, female body strode out.

"I can't believe you ditched the party, Matt," Amy Byrd cooed. "I was looking for you all night."

"I'll catch up with Paul to do some guy things," Matt said dismissively then bid her a hasty good-bye. She stood open-mouthed at his brusqueness as he made his way over to Molly's desk.

"Hi. Thought I might take the woman of the hour out for a real date," he said loudly enough for Amy to hear. "How about dinner and a movie?"

A real date! Molly couldn't hide her joy. Was he asking her out just to get rid of Amy? No, she didn't think so. Her face flushed with radiance as she accepted. Amy Byrd stormed off in a huff, but neither Matt nor Molly gave her any notice.

"Look." Molly waved her check. "Let me take *you* to dinner. I don't have extra money too often." She told Matt about her surprise bonus.

"You can buy me pizza some other time. You need to treat yourself to something special with that money. You deserve it after the month you've had. Let's see, how about a shopping spree, a day at the spa, a weekend in the Outer Banks . . ."

"Actually, I was thinking of taking a class over at the Cultural Arts Center."

Matt smiled and picked up her work bag as they headed out to the front door. Outside, sheets of rain fell on the warm ground as steam sprang up from the concrete sidewalks. Matt opened a large golf umbrella and beckoned Molly to join him under its protective cover. "But you're already smarter than all of us," he teased. "What kind of class?"

"The kind that starts Friday." Molly turned a beaming face up to his and called loudly over the beating rain, "It's called Pottery for Beginners."

· · ·

Rookie officer Monica Clarke was irritated that she was always assigned the job of fetching and sorting the police station's mail. Organizing a stack of letters and catalogues for Officer Bennett, Monica noticed that the current edition of his weekly sports magazine featured swimsuit models instead of football players.

"Men," she muttered, cramming Bennett's mail together in a sloppy pile. If Bennett asked her to get him another cup of coffee she would threaten to sue on grounds of gender discrimination. Little did Monica know that Officer McLeary, a large, muscular African-American man, had also been forced to fetch coffee for Bennett before he was allowed to work the beat. All the rookies started off doing desk work, and they had all gotten Bennett coffee, regardless of gender.

Monica also wasn't aware of the existence of a small envelope addressed in neat handwriting to Officer Bennett. It was from a woman named Molly Appleby. Shoved between the pages of his sports magazine, the missive was completely hidden from view.

Bennett looked up from a thick, uneven stack of paperwork as Monica entered the room. He groaned at the sight of his pile of mail and knew he would never be free to take his new bride out for lunch.

He brightened when he shifted through the pile and his gaze fell upon the lithe tanned body of a brunette in a white string bikini. He gazed furtively at the cover, knowing that his possessive wife would not approve of him ogling other women, even airbrushed ones.

Bennett was just about to settle down to a leisurely viewing of a dozen swimsuit models when he heard the familiar clipping of high-heeled shoes and a perky, bright voice moving through the station's main room.

His lovely bride would reach his office in seconds. In a blind panic, Bennett shoved the magazine into the paper shredder and pressed it down firmly into the biting metal teeth. As his wife stepped into the office, picnic basket in hand, her fiery red hair and wide smile quickly made Bennett forget all about swimsuit models.

Along with a letter detailing the death of a notorious collector, the models had all become narrow, feathery ribbons of scrap paper.

• • •

The clay sank into the wheel like an old man dropping into a deep, soft chair. The mouth of the bowl spun into a lopsided yawn that seemed to mock the young hands upon its smooth, wet body.

The potter placed his hands over the boy's, cupping the bowl until the walls sprang high again. The clay recognized the tie between the two sets of hands and began to respect the strength of their union. Together, they forced it to behave with all the love and firmness of a father.

The door to the shed opened and the potter's wife brought in tall, sweating glasses of lemonade. The potter drank the sugary sunlight and smiled in contentment.

Alone, the small hands held the clay steady for a few more turns of the wheel before the bowl keeled over to one side like a sinking ship. The child looked pleadingly at the potter.

Reshaping the fallen clay into a firm ball, the potter replaced it on the wheel. He patted his son on the back and held his shoulders as it began to spin.

"You can make another," he told him gently, his voice filled with pride.

The potter was right. He would make another. And another.

He would make thousands.

A Brief Note on Face Jugs

Faces have been given to ceramic vessels throughout history. From Egyptian canobic jars to English toby mugs, face vessels have appeared across the centuries in a multitude of cultures. Though no one knows for certain *why* the first American face jugs were created, historians do know *where* these fascinating objects began to be produced with regularity.

In the western part of South Carolina, in a region called Edgefield, several potters created face jugs, also referred to as "ugly jugs" during the middle of the nineteenth century.

Many of these potters were African Americans. These jugs or bottles were turned in the regular manner, and then decorated with applied eyes and horizontal bits of teeth often made with unglazed porcelain. Over time, the subjects of these clay portraits have been lost to us, creating a sense of mystery around each nameless face vessel with its two eyes, two ears, a nose, a mouth, and rows of teeth. One thing is definitive, however, and that is that no two face jugs are alike.

In the early part of the twentieth century, face jugs were not a common part of the Southern potter's bread-and-butter sales. During the 1930s, several North Carolina potters began to produce face vessels to sell, but were still relying on their traditional utilitarian wares to support their families. Eventually, technological advancements allowed for the mass production of ceramic ware, and the individual potter either packed it in or found a new attraction to keep his customers returning. For some potters, this attraction was the face jug. Hoping to appeal to tourists, potters spent a great deal of extra time creating a lifelike face or at least one unique enough to catch the eye of a customer.

In the 1960s and 1970s, more and more Southern potters began creating face jugs for the tourist trade. Though especially prolific in North Carolina and Georgia, potters throughout the United States made faces on jugs, cups, pitchers, vases, and a variety of other vessels. In the last few decades, those faces have gotten fancy too. Examples such as the female face, war-painted Native Americans, devils, Medusas, and even animal face vessels have been introduced into the mix. Some potters have also made two-faced jugs, with one side being a devil and the other an angel, a man and a woman, a happy and a sad face, or a two-faced, irreverent representation of the politician.

The face jug has been called "grotesque" in the past and it is true— many are a bit daunting with their pointed teeth, bleeding eyes, long fangs, or devil horns. But the face jug is an excellent example of how an art form can be created in a few workshops in one area in the country, and then slowly appear in other regions. For whatever reason that first American face vessel was made, whether for religious or ritualistic purposes, as a gift, or simply as an artistic experiment, the face jug was born to be embraced by thousands of artists and collectors.

About the Author

Ellery Adams, a *USA Today* and *New York Times* bestselling author, has written dozens of mystery novels. She shares her North Carolina home with her husband, two trolls, and three keyboard-hogging felines. Ellery loves reading, coffee, bubbly, jigsaw puzzles, baking, volunteering at her local animal shelter, and rearranging her bookshelves.

Her traditionally published series include The Secret, Book, and Scone Society Mysteries, The Book Retreat Mysteries, The Books By the Bay Mysteries, and The Charmed Pie Shoppe Mysteries.

Her Indie series include The Supper Club Mysteries, The Hope Street Church Mysteries, and The Antiques & Collectibles Mysteries.

For book club discussion questions, lists of Nora Pennington's bibliotherapy titles, and more, visit www.elleryadamsmysteries.com.

Made in the USA
Middletown, DE
13 April 2023

28804541R00111